LAST NOTES and other stories

Tamas Dobozy

Last Notes and other stories

 HarperCollinsPublishersLtd
A PHYLLIS BRUCE BOOK

First edition

HarperCollins books may be purchased for educational, business,
or sales promotional use through our Special Markets Department.

HarperCollins Publishers Ltd
2 Bloor Street East, 20th Floor
Toronto, Ontario, Canada
M4W 1A8

www.harpercollins.ca

Library and Archives Canada Cataloguing in Publication

Dobozy, Tamas, 1969–
Last notes : and other stories / Tamas Dobozy.

Short stories.
"A Phyllis Bruce Book".
ISBN-13: 978-0-00-200590-6
ISBN-10: 0-00-200590-5

I. Title.

PS8557.O2218L38 2005   C813'.54   C2004-907087-8

HC 9 8 7 6 5 4 3 2 1

Printed and bound in the United States
Set in Minion and Akzidenz Grotesk

For all my second homes:

Éva Cserei
Gigi and Ildi Galter
Bea and Laci Korányi
Kati Csizér
Bandi Dobozy

And in memory:

Gábor Galter (1909–2004)
Endre Dobozy (1899–1946)
Piroska Dobozy (1910–1962)

Contents

Tales of Hungarian Resistance

THE AGENTS of the Arrow Cross Party arrested my grandfather on October 25, 1944. They found him at the Turul, a butcher shop notorious for having no fixed address—a place that would pop up, open for a few weeks, disappear, and then re-open in a district not under attack, following a string of addresses coveted by all but known only to an extremely exclusive, violent, and black-shirted clientele. Here there were pork chops for sale, and steak, even filet mignon if your timing was right—and none of that stuff everyone else had to eat, grey-green and scavenged from downed cavalry regiments, so riddled with bullets and shrapnel it was known as "metal meat." According to my grandfather, he was inspecting a rod of salami when the SS marched in and carried him off to the Andrássy út prison, where he remained until news of Hungary's imminent defeat allowed him to slip past the distracted prison guards and haul his body—ravaged by six months of interrogation—through the shattered streets to where my grandmother lived.

From this point, another story begins—that of my family's trials throughout the years of Communism—but that is not what I am speaking of now. No, the event that concerns my grandfather, and by extension me, is that half-year he spent behind a thick wooden door, surrounded by stone walls, hemmed in by fences and barbed wire, while Nazi interrogators worked him over for information on the "Titkos Magyar Szövetség"—the "Secret Hungarian Union"—a group of partisans either invented by my grandfather or imagined by the Nazis, and which, for the purposes of this story, I will simply call the "Hungarian Resistance."

We all know about the French Underground. They are celebrated

1

in films and history books and novels. We know of the Polish Secret State and the Polish Home Army and their terrible betrayal by Stalin and the Soviet forces during the Warsaw Uprising in the summer of 1944. And maybe the best thing about the publicity and respect lavished on these men and women—their sacrifices, their subversion—is that it leaves a little less room in history for some of the more ambiguous aspects of World War II, such as Hungary's opportunistic relations with the Nazis, either during Horthy Miklós's nationalist dictatorship from 1920 to 1944—when he agreed to pass anti-Semitic laws in return for territory lost through the Treaty of Trianon—or during Ferenc Szálasi and the Arrow Cross Party's government, imposed on the country by the Nazis near the end of the war. It's true that, in late 1944, a bunch of disaffected military men got together and formed an illegal organization called the "Committee of Liberation," which lasted maybe two months before it was discovered and its general staff all imprisoned and tortured and executed; and it's true that, around the same time, a related organization, known as the "Independence Front" formed in eastern Hungary, an unlikely alliance of remnants from Horthy's administration, communists, and social democrats, united only in their hatred of the Arrow Cross Party. But there was no early and rigorous opposition to Hungary's alliance with Nazi Germany. And when opposition did come, it was less out of hostility to the national and racial chauvinism of Horthy and Szálasi than simply a desire to exit a war Hungary was losing. So, if this story asks a question, I suppose it's this: Were my grandfather's tales of the Hungarian Resistance an attempt to erase this "troubling fact"—in an act of patriotic revisionism—or rather to correct it?

If you listen to my grandmother, who's outlived her husband by ten years, his stories were bullshit, complete bullshit, from beginning to end. Of course, I know what my grandfather would say, if he could sit up in his grave and get the worms out of his mouth for a second; he'd say the subtleties of the form that resistance took escape her, because with her German temperament and upbringing she's unable to appreciate anything *as resistance* that isn't all-out assault. But she has outlived him, and I guess that's a victory of sorts, one that lets her have the last word on what happened. In the end, she knows more about resistance than he ever did.

About the background, there's little you need know. In 1943, Admiral Horthy, witnessing the terrible casualties inflicted on his armies by the Russians at the Battle of the Don, began "adjusting" his relations with his "ally," Germany, and his "enemies," the Allied Powers—adjustments that eventually came to the attention of Adolf Hitler, and culminated in Horthy's displacement in 1944 by Szálasi and the Arrow Cross Party, a group of rabid pro-Nazis who made up for Horthy's July 7 decision to stop the deportation of Hungarian Jews by quickly sending another thirty thousand to Auschwitz. My grandmother recalls how those Jews who remained were herded into the Danube and shot, left to float downstream and snag on the bridges connecting Buda to Pest, so that walking across you saw bodies swirling in the eddies around pilings and foundations, most of them on their backs, the bullet holes in their foreheads looking up like eyes singular, cyclopean—the only gaze equal to a sky raining bullets and flame.

It was Szálasi who employed a man by the name of Ákos Mennyászky, an expert interrogator who was to prove my grandfather's most frequent visitor at Andrássy út prison.

To this day, Mennyászky is still the person I sympathize with, still the image I find peering at me from shop windows, pools of water, mirrors—the haunting figure who glides through my brain, ransacking the memories of my grandfather for hidden compartments, for the real information that will let him close the case and go home for the day. But there's nothing to fasten onto, no memory that isn't suspect. And after all that grandfather and I went through, after all the explanations and accusations, the only legacy that remains is this sympathy for a Nazi who, like me, starved for lack of evidence, losing himself in the act of seeking an impossible verification. I am haunted by Mennyászky because his obsession is my obsession, because I am, like him, not able to trust my information, and because I have become my grandfather's interrogator.

Mennyászky was blasé about his job, and so his co-workers hated him. They'd seen all sorts of interrogators: vicious bastards like Klaus Barbie, who went into the chamber more enthusiastic about the way they were going to get the information than about the information itself, or quiet men like Hans Scharff, who became friends with every prisoner they ever questioned. But Mennyászky wasn't like either of these—neither psychotic nor sympathetic; he never saw his work in metaphysical terms, as a higher calling. In fact, most of the time he seemed as tired and disgruntled as if he'd been filing papers for the last ten years in some mid-level bureaucracy. Even while someone's fingers were being broken or his skin broiled with torches, his face showed the boredom and absentmindedness you might have seen on a clerk inserting numbers into a ledger. He was often caught sneaking out of work early, and so he'd be turned around, going back in his hangdog fashion— "Okay, okay, I'll give you another ten minutes . . ."—back to the room from which screams would shortly issue, only to emerge again at five o'clock, right on the button, often leaving the informant in mid-sentence—cut off in the act of finally revealing what they'd been trying to pry from him all these weeks and months— and saying "Quitting time is quitting time" when the commanding officer reprimanded him. If not for his perfect record at cracking recalcitrant prisoners, they'd have relocated him to the front years ago. His dreams, Mennyászky's colleagues said, were as dusty and shopworn as a pair of old, comfortable shoes.

...

Before I go further, I suppose I should provide another context for the telling of the tale. Mostly, I heard this story in the summertime, when my grandfather would awaken from his winter depressions and start talking again, and take me into the back garden of the Budapest apartment building where we lived. He'd sit on a folding chair under an elderflower tree, with me squatting at his feet, and repeat the long, elaborate narrative in between swilling five to six bottles of beer. Meanwhile, my grandmother would come up behind him and inject little bits of commentary alongside his narrative—lines of marginalia. For instance, when he described his return from the Andrássy út prison—his wasted body, his bare and bleeding feet, his shaved head—she would say, "You were as fat and pampered as a pig for slaughter." When he recalled how he'd talked and talked, feeding the Nazis long strings of misinformation, she'd turn and say, "You gave them everything they wanted, and so they gave you clean carpet slippers and roast turkey and all the potatoes you could stuff into your gullet." And when he repeated, for the two hundredth time, how he had beaten the most skilled interrogator in the history of Hungary, she would turn away, shaking her head: "You became his best friend."

My grandmother's problem, of course, was that she had no story—only a commentary. Without my grandfather and his tales she could say nothing. And I suspect that her unwillingness to go beyond these snide comments, to fully articulate the extent of grandfather's guilt, even after all the condemnation heaped on him between 1945 and 1990—when he was briefly imprisoned again in a gulag, denied proper status under the Soviet regime, barred from employment and party membership—was partly because he had consistently maintained his innocence and partly because she *wanted* to believe in what he said, *wanted* to feel that all those years of sacrifice—when she worked triple time just to keep the family going—hadn't been wasted on a traitor.

My grandfather, meanwhile, had, from the time I was old enough to understand a sentence, my undivided attention. It was only later, after that incident in the doctor's office, that cracks started to appear in his story, and my grandmother's lament changed from a background noise into something integral to the tale, leaving me with the same kind of doubts that must have followed Mennyászky home after his long sessions in the torture chamber.

It went like this. My grandfather maintained that the SS had been tailing him for days—ever since his last meeting with the Resistance (to which the Nazis had been tipped off by an informant)—before they finally apprehended him in the butcher shop (conversely, my grandmother held that he was just in the wrong place at the wrong time, and that the Nazis got lucky). Realizing that they were taking him to the Andrássy út prison, and that they would try to get from him everything he knew, my grandfather decided on a unique strategy: instead of heroically holding out, maintaining a resolute silence through the beatings and electrocutions and fingernail removals, and instead of just giving them everything they wanted right up front, he decided to give them more information than they could handle.

I can just see Mennyászky getting out of bed that April morning, waiting until the last possible second to pop out from under the covers, jump in the shower, slurp down his coffee, thinking all the while that it would be another routine day of torture. Instead, he was to face the biggest babbler of his life.

Their first meeting was meant to occur in silence. This was Mennyászky's standard introduction: enter the room with a cohort of five blackshirts, sit across the table from the prisoner, stare at him for six or seven hours, and then get up and walk out. There would follow a night of such terror—the prisoner feeling the interrogator's eyes on him even in the dark—and of such apprehension for the next day, that sometimes Mennyászky's job would be over by sunrise. But my grandfather, the minute Mennyászky sank into his seat across the table, said, "Hello. My real name is Sándor Balázs. Here are the names of some of my associates in the Hungarian Resistance: Györffy Pál, Kovács Ferenc, Horváth Géza, and Mester Anikó. I would also like to present you with a series of addresses. Please listen carefully, and note the following . . ."

He hadn't even given Mennyászky a chance to engage the glare.

And so my grandfather let it go, all of it, inventing endless reams of information, spreading it around, hour upon hour, inexhaustibly. Mennyászky sat there impassive; he'd seen this before, seen these raconteurs come in, not so much scared of the torture as happy to finally have an audience who *had* to listen to them, pathologically grateful for the presence of the interrogator. Meanwhile, the stenographer sat on the other side of the wall, behind all those holes drilled for sound, feverishly typing on a roll of paper, converting that confessional stream into marks on a page, something for the men back at intelligence to scratch their heads over.

And scratch their heads they did. By the end of that first night, my grandfather had broken all previous records for torture-room confessions, and by a huge margin, a record all the more notable for the fact that not one single torture implement had come into play, not even a threat. That night—where nobody in the room apart from my grandfather, who stopped only to moisten his throat, had uttered a word—produced an unprecedented one hundred pages of information.

Mennyászky was incredulous. While he'd never witnessed such a volume of material, he'd faced (or thought he had) many prisoners of this type. In fact, he was so dismissive he didn't even bother to review the material my grandfather had provided, simply packing up as usual at five o'clock and heading out, regarding the evening as a less than satisfactory start toward getting the true confession.

So he was surprised the next day coming in to work. His commanding officer, Hans Liebing, took him aside and said that after Mennyászky had left, another interrogator had taken over, and the confession had continued into the morning. A double-team of intelligence men had spent the night verifying the information provided by my grandfather and had discovered that there were some "anomalies" amidst the general babble—fragments, innocuous clauses—that had turned out, upon investigation, to be true, including directions to a trapdoor in an apartment in the ninth district that opened on a room filled with communications equipment and reports from the Allies, to a cache of scavenged weapons in an unused tool alcove in the Budapest sewers, and to the home of an eighty-year-old woman, by then deceased, who had a trunk full of materials used to forge identity cards. After these first few discoveries, they dispatched agents to track down each of my grandfather's "leads," and reports were still coming in, 99 percent of them negative, but, every other hour or so, there was the discovery of something legitimate.

Liebing had never had much luck with Mennyászky, largely because he couldn't figure the man out. He was so ordinary. But on this morning he made himself clear: "Listen, Mennyászky, this guy obviously knows things, but I can't paralyze this department by verifying and tracking down every lead he gives us; you've got to figure out some way to make him leave out what's made up and give us the truth."

And the department *was* paralyzed. Mennyászky saw it that morning, the bags under the eyes of his co-workers, the guards and agents impatient and fidgety from lack of sleep, the piles of used coffee grounds in the cafeteria garbage cans. All attention had been diverted away from the other political prisoners and focused exclusively on my grandfather.

Mennyászky had never come up against anything like this. In his experience there were two types: the ones who spewed garbage until the screws were really applied, at which point the truth came screaming out; or the silent individuals who either died prior to revealing anything or became vegetables who'd tell you whatever you wanted to know—in their soft, monotonous way. And he was used to two types of confession—non-fiction and fiction—his job being to force the prisoner from one genre into another. But never, in all the years spent in the torture chamber, had he encountered such hybrid intelligence, this fugue of imagination and fact. Mennyászky could turn a man into a confessor or a corpse, but he had yet to turn anyone into an editor.

I still picture him wandering the streets of the gutted capital, one eye out for bombing raids overhead, his hand over his stomach as if there were a piece of shrapnel lodged there, or, perhaps for the first time, a hint of obsession, a need to finally put in some over-time, an inability to get farther than a few blocks from the prison even when the commanding officer ordered him home for a rest.

According to my grandfather, Mennyászky put an exclusive voucher in on him, meaning that no other interrogator was allowed access. And over the six months of their "relationship"—and they were tireless as lovers in eliciting responses from one another with-out giving away too much of themselves—Mennyászky tried any number of strategies to get him to speak. For instance, he'd have my grandfather stop after every revelation, try and force him to be silent while he sent out one of his boys to check on it, then applying several minutes of extreme pain to the prisoner if the news turned out to be phony, only then asking the next question—hoping, in this way, to get my grandfather to pare away the inconsistencies, the evasions, *the stories*, and just speak the truth. The only problem was, of course, that while they were torturing him, my grandfather would howl out a dozen more bits of information—all of which had to be verified, because, once in a while, one of these bits would turn out to be crucial to the Axis cause.

Then, Mennyászky himself tried becoming an editor, spending long nights poring over the transcripts of the torture sessions, looking for some giveaway, some stylistic tic that would help him differentiate a confession from a lie. But my grandfather's mode of telling was too mixed, and Mennyászky discovered, with a sour delight, that the man must have read a lot of literature, because there were all manner of forms present, masked by the rushed voice, the near-scream in which the sentences were delivered. He found information on an alleged underground newspaper delivered in a brilliant alliteration. He found whole paragraphs in flawless iambic pentameter, which was not a rhythm that came easily to Hungarian. He found an oration on the modes of sabotage employed by the Resistance delivered in a pastiche of Szálasi's public address. But there was no consistency to the quality of information, and a bit of truth delivered in literary form one day might be murmured idiomatically the next. It is said that around this time Mennyászky started losing his hair.

According to my grandfather, this went on for six months, his tongue working a groove into the roof of his mouth with the incessant monologues he delivered, spicing the stories here and there with bits of truth, but revealing nothing—and my grandfather swears to this—truly damaging to the Hungarian Resistance: mainly just locations of supplies the partisans had already been cut off from, by bombing, building collapse, police cordons thrown up by the Arrow Cross; details of hideouts already discovered or destroyed or abandoned; names of the dead or arrested, or those who had switched sides. And none of Mennyászky's tactics ever succeeded in making him give selective information, or anything truly incriminating.

And this was pretty much my grandfather's story, though of course I've left out the bits where he would dazzle me by re-enacting, sometimes for hours, the kinds of soliloquies he'd delivered, rapid-fire accounts of places and faces—almost too rich, too ornate, to take in—and which veered from inventories of equipment and food to digressions on ideology and interpartisan rivalries, to anecdotes on bravery and self-sacrifice, like some soap opera whose strands he could pick up at any time, juggling three dozen characters whose relationships with each other and with the enemy seemed to be progressing toward some terrible resolution, but one that was always delayed. At times I would stand in front of the mirror and pretend I was facing Mennyászky and attempt to deliver a similar monologue, but I always stalled after five or six sentences, as if the gap between my imagination and mouth had grown too large for the stories to leap. In the end, I could not put myself in grandfather's place.

But eventually, as I grew older and more aware, it was my grand-mother's commentary that commanded my attention. At times, she suggested that the SS arrested my grandfather only because he hap-pened to be in a shop frequented by Horthy's top brass (who, by the time of the Arrow Cross, were being rounded up and charged with sedition). So maybe somebody had told him about the butcher's, and he'd chosen to go on the wrong day. Maybe it was an accident.

You see, my grandfather had worked for the Horthy administra-tion before and during the war—as had my father—and my grandmother suspected, in line with official reports later released by the Soviets, that grandfather had betrayed his fellow partisans, Bajcsy-Zsilinszky and General Kiss, in return for certain "domestic comforts." So, my father's murder, and my mother's disappear-ance, along with the liquidation of the other leaders of the Committee of Liberation, might very well have been a result of information leaked by my grandfather—making his willingness to raise me as much an act of guilt as an act of love.

My grandfather, of course, denied all accusations. He swore he never had anything to do with the Committee, never mind plot-ting to betray them, and that all his activities were restricted to the Hungarian Resistance (a group, if it existed at all, so nebulous, so careful not to leave a document or witness, that I've yet to find any-thing to verify it). There were other times, however, when my grandfather's story shimmered with subtext—a faint light beneath a troubled, *and troubling*, surface of water—a hint, a bare sugges-tion, that maybe he'd invented the Resistance altogether, either to leave Mennyászky one failure in an otherwise spotless record, or to give himself enough subject matter for a six-month-long confession, or—and this is the most noble of his suggestions—for the sake of the Committee of Liberation itself, to throw the Nazis off the trail of an organization that had recruited both his daughter and son-in-law. But he never came out and said it.

And so the man I wanted to track down all those years, when I still craved certainty, was Mennyászky. He was the only one who could tell me whether my grandfather had spent those six months in agony, giving false witness, or whether he'd spent that time as a pampered guest of the SS—all that fine wine and dining—in return for an ever-increasing list of names, including those of my parents.

I think the moment when my grandmother's voice emerged from the background and became a central part of my consciousness took place on that fall afternoon when I accompanied my grandfather to the hospital. I was twelve.

We waited a considerable time, as always, in the worn front room of the St. John's Infirmary, watching patients shuffle back and forth in striped pyjamas—inmates in yet another institution. After a bit, a nurse came out and ushered us into a small room with a bed, a cupboard, and jars of medical implements. A few minutes later the specialist, a small man whose body looked far older than his eyes, and who seemed to be constantly jerking forward, as if to throw off something clinging to his back, entered the room. He began by taking my grandfather's blood pressure, making notes, palpating his veins, testing the reflexes below each knee.

It was when the doctor asked my grandfather to open his mouth and say "ah" that he recognized him. And here he stopped. Then he pulled his head back and spat directly into my grandfather's face.

I can barely remember what happened next—so shocked was I by the treatment given a man for whom I had nothing but respect—but it involved a torrent of abuse from the doctor, who'd remembered my grandfather from recent newspaper articles, and who, it turned out, had suffered under the Arrow Cross, either by being put into a ghetto, or sent to a concentration camp, or implicated in some anti-Nazi plot and tortured. "You are a coward, and a traitor not only to your country but your family. And you are not worth the five minutes I have just wasted on you." The doctor spat on him once again before walking out.

Somehow we made it home, though I remember that both of us were in such a daze we could hardly figure out which buses to board, which streetcar to transfer to, and that my grandfather, who'd just looked at the floor the whole time the doctor went at him, still had the spit, shining, on his cheeks. My grandmother, who greeted us at the door, immediately sensed that something was wrong, and she pulled us apart, sending me to my room where I lay on the bed, stared at the picture of my parents on the wall over the headboard, and finally started to register what my grandmother had been saying, under her breath, all these years. *My grandfather was a liar. A storyteller.*

Nonetheless, she tried to soften the trauma, taking me aside the next morning and saying that a lot of people had mixed-up ideas about my grandfather, and that I shouldn't take them seriously, since nobody, not even she, really knew what had gone on at the Andrássy út prison. But by then I was all suspicion, and couldn't figure out whose innocence she was protecting—my grandfather's or mine.

And for several years, almost two decades in fact, I did everything I could to find out what really happened. I had several confrontations with my grandfather, who held fast to his story, and which ultimately soured our relationship, with me angry at him for holding out, and him unable to understand why, after being urged to confess the truth, and having confessed it, he was never left in peace. I enrolled in university, studying political science and history; I did graduate work in the West; I was granted access to certain select releases from the KGB archives. None of this helped clarify that period in my grandfather's life.

And when I tried tracking down Mennyászky, I came up against emptiness. He was shipped off to a gulag after the war ended, and survived, later becoming rehabilitated and rejoining society as a "useful but quiet comrade" in a mining enterprise outside Miskolc. He never again put his peculiar talent to use, as if he'd finally achieved the ordinariness that had been his calling card. The few relatives and neighbours still willing to speak of Mennyászky confirmed that a kind of stillness had settled over him, that he would frequently be seen walking to or from work, or just out for the day, along the fences and gardens bordering the streets, his eyes always averted from passersby and staring straight at the ground, minutely inspecting everything that passed beneath his feet, as might a man who's just discovered a hole in his pocket, or lost some heirloom or letter, something without which he finds it impossible to stand still, to sit at a table and eat, or to sleep. I like to think of Mennyászky still worrying over the Hungarian Resistance, whether or not it had actually existed. Though probably he was just lost, unable to figure out how he'd gotten so turned around in history in so short a time.

And after a while I just stopped thinking about it. No, that's too easy a description. What happened is that my thinking shifted, away from the intangibles swirling around my grandfather, to what I could be sure of, to what there was some agreement upon, my grandmother and what she'd endured: the triple shifts, the shaming and ostracizing of her family, the humiliating efforts to regain some standing in society, sucking up to various low-level party members so that her children and grandchildren could get jobs, or even, maybe, entry to a university. Here was something reliable, not because there was documentation to prove it, or fingerprints, or any of that standard evidence, but because she was willing to stand behind it, willing to take both the blame and praise for whatever happened—to offer no excuses. And that willingness, finally, is what I've come to understand as history.

Though I must say that I still wake up some nights with the events of 1944 playing in my head in all their ambiguity. At times I am tempted to think of my grandfather as a murderer, at times as a saviour. Mostly, though, I just think of my grandmother, that woman who was willing to sacrifice her life to an illusion the old man needed, no matter how the solitude weighed upon her, no matter how many people told her to abandon him, to take a new name, to start over. This was her act of resistance, and it was, in a way, no less heroic than anything dreamed up in the underground. And on such nights I will get up from bed and go to the bathroom for a glass of water, or to take a piss, or to shower the sweat from my body.

Then, I'll sit for a while in front of the mirror, thinking of those terrible afternoons under the elderflower tree in the garden, when all the world was a story I could readily believe. And I'll wonder what is worse: taking the stand that is history, that is a willingness to say you've done wrong and that maybe there is no way to make amends; or, being so afraid of what's back there, waiting behind you in the dark, that you cut yourself loose from all history to see how long you can survive in the thin air, kicked free into a lightness that is also ghostliness, where you have no bearings, no relation to what's gone or going on, and where everything you encounter passes through you like a wind in the chambers of the heart.

I'll sit weighing this thought for a while, and then I'll go back to bed.

Dead Letters

MY FIRST IMPULSE was to warn Oscar that he might get arrested. My second, of course, was to see some of the stuff he was selling. And Oscar reached for his mail sack, from where he sat sipping beer in the sunshine of my back deck, and pulled out a bunch of postcards held together with elastics. But before handing them over he stopped and asked, "You're not Christian, are you?"

Naturally I lied, telling him my father had been a hardcore socialist, and my mother descended from a long line of what were once called freethinkers. This caused Oscar to pause for a minute, look at me as if I were a dolt, and then shrug and hand over the package of postcards.

I slipped the elastics off and started quickly flipping through them, gradually slowing as I went from one postcard to the next until stopping at number twelve, which showed Christ, arms akimbo, dangling painfully from a crucifix. It was a standard pose except that some guy had pasted a picture of his own face over Christ's, and that this face, obviously cut from a snapshot, was licking an ice cream cone. I flipped back and wondered how I could have missed it: the same face pasted onto each of the fourteen postcards. Instead of Veronica wiping Jesus's face, you had her pressing a veil to the face of a man who had the stem of a beer bottle attached to his mouth. Instead of the Roman legionnaire bringing a rod down on Christ's back, he was beating someone wearing a straw fedora. Instead of the usual limp and drained and gaping-mouthed Christ in the figure of the *Pietà*, you had a man smiling around an enormous cigar. "These are the Stations of the Cross," I said, trying to hide my surprise.

Oscar shrugged and turned and sipped his drink, the noon sun-shine glancing off the buttons and epaulets of his mail-carrier's uniform. I was drinking coffee, because for me it was still morning, while Oscar, who regularly woke at 3 a.m. to get out and deliver the mail, was well into what he called his "darkness at noon," which meant that, for him, night began the instant the last letter had been delivered. His bedtime was only five hours away.

I turned over the postcards and noted they had all been written by someone called Robert, and were all addressed to someone called Roger, and that they were, without exception, filled with the usual drivel you find on postcards: "Jerusalem is lovely this time of year"; "Hey, I think I'm really getting to appreciate Jewish food"; "Man, you ought to see the women around here"; etc.

"How much do you get for this stuff?" I asked Oscar. He shrugged and swigged on his beer and said it depended entirely on his contact, who would spread the word among the collectors and then get back to him with a number of offers. Then Oscar would either accept one of these offers or tell his contact they were all too low, hoping to start a bidding war. I looked through the postcards again and wondered who would pay money for this sick stuff. Oscar responded by saying that this kind of "stuff" rarely went for big money because most dead-letter collectors preferred unopened mail and packages, since it was the thrill of the unknown that made them "fetish objects."

"You're telling me there's people out there who will pay money to open other people's mail?" I handed the postcards back to Oscar, who replaced the elastic bands and dropped them back into his mail sack. He grabbed another beer out of the cooler I kept on my back deck and said it wasn't opening up other people's mail that provided the thrill, but opening letters that no longer had owners, that couldn't be delivered at all because the sender and addressee were no longer locatable. Letters that were stalled in the space between delivery and return. The collectors' interest wasn't so much voyeurism, peering into someone else's life, as impersonation, tak-ing on that life, becoming the person the letters were sent to.

"I don't get it," I said. "What's so great about that?"

"Well," said Oscar, "that's what makes it a fetish, right? I mean, if it was normal behaviour then you probably would have heard about it by now." It was hard to argue with this, though it didn't make things any clearer. "It's like saving someone from extinction," said Oscar. "You keep their information alive." I shrugged my shoulders, and he waved his hand at me. "Forget it," he said.

Eventually, Oscar did go to jail, for ten months, and I narrowly escaped being called in as a material witness and being charged as an accessory, after Oscar confessed. What did end up happening, though, was that I was fired from my job as mail-sorter technician at Canada Post. And my EI ran out a few weeks before Oscar got out of jail.

I had visited him once, just long enough to tell him I wasn't too impressed with his friendship. He replied to this by ignoring me and going on at length about how jail was pretty cushy, with a bunch of pool tables, a tennis court, and an arts and crafts centre. Nonetheless, Oscar said, despite these "perks," he couldn't shake the nightmares he was having, that prisons were really no different from the dead-letter office in the postal warehouse, all those stacks and stacks of misdirected mail sitting there gathering dust, waiting for the statute of limitations to expire so they could become property of the state, which meant, for most of them, immediate incineration. "What am I going to do when I get out?" Oscar asked. "All I've ever done is carry mail." I hung up the phone in disgust after reminding Oscar that I had far more right to be asking that question of him than he had to be asking it of me.

My mother, of course, had *her* explanation. After I recounted the story, including the part about looking at the postcards, she peppered me with questions: Had I "lingered" over the postcards? Had

I laughed? Had I made even a token attempt to remove the blasphemous pasted-over pictures of the guy's face from that of "our Lord"? Had I, even for one second, considered doing the "right thing" and turning over Oscar to the "proper authorities"? Had I thought back over the postcards in the days since and perhaps been "tempted" to smile, or laugh, or, God forbid, play such a "blasphemous joke" myself?

"Mother," I replied, staring at the floor, "I've just lost my job. Please tell me, what on earth have the postcards to do with that?" She shook her head and started interrogating me about when I'd last gone to church; and whether I still did my "minimum duty" in attending and receiving communion at Easter Sunday mass; and, moreover, what kind of relationship I had, exactly, with that "good for nothing pervert," Oscar. "*Relationship?* Mother, we're friends. We *were* friends." But this did not satisfy her, and she kept poking the long fingers of her inquiry into me, rooting around in my conscience the way a surgeon pulls aside the membranes and organs of a patient undergoing exploratory surgery, hoping to find that big lump of cancer she just knew was there. This had been her primary occupation since my father died and I moved out, the two events that had come to define her moral universe—though she pretended her perspective was all Saint Augustine.

"Why is it, Mother," I asked, "that when something good happens to me you say it's the work of providence, but when something bad happens it's always my fault? Has it ever occurred to you that maybe it's the other way around? Maybe the good things are due to me, and maybe the bad things are God's fault."

"That is exactly the sort of thing your father would have said," she replied, the expression on her face more like an upside-down smile than a real frown, a displeasure that made her happy.

Naturally, my father did not attend mass. I remember heading out the door with my mother on Sunday mornings and looking back at him standing there in our kitchen, the only time he would ever wear an apron, holding a giant spatula up in the air and yelling out—more for the benefit of my mother, though he always pretended to be speaking to me—his standard "excuse" for not accompanying us to church: "Hey, little buddy, someone's got to stay home and cook breakfast!" I could hear him laughing at this joke every single week, the sound carrying until the bells of Saint Patrick's came into hearing.

But when we got home from church—after what seemed to my child's ears a repetitive sermon; followed by that lining up for a wafer so unappetizing my mother had to keep reminding me of the medallions I'd get just to keep me interested in first holy communion; followed by the chit-chat she indulged in once mass was over—after all *that*, we'd get home and there would be Father standing in front of an enormous spread of sausages and waffles and eggs and peameal bacon and hash browns and fruit salad and freshly squeezed orange juice, all the things I'd been salivating after throughout mass.

I'd run into the kitchen, slip off my tie and the itchy, tight, polyester suit jacket my mother had bought, and jump up beside my plate, thinking that if I was the first one to put my hands together for grace I'd also be the first one to take them apart and grab a knife and fork.

After grace, which my father would watch with a bemused detachment, we'd dig in, Father spearing massive oily sausages, heaping his plate with mounds of hash browns he drowned in ketchup, surreptitiously stealing bits of strawberry from the fruit salad (a practice he called "highgrading," and which he vociferously condemned when anyone else did it). And the whole time he ate and dumped food on our plates, he would be turning to my mother with every spoonful, every lifting of the fork, every return to the stove for more, and begging her to pardon his "gluttony," until his joy at being able to provide us with such a feast overcame her (it had long overcome me) and she would break into a grin, and finally laugh. In the end, my mother would simply shake her head and giggle, "Henry, you're such an idiot." And then the seriousness of my father's face would also break, and he'd smile back at her in such a way that I would realize, seemingly for the first time every Sunday, that he was not at all competing with her, or with the church, for my affection, but was just trying to celebrate our time together.

But since he was dead by the time I lost my job at Canada Post, it was my mother who agreed to "help out." Unfortunately, this meant I had to move back in with her, which meant living with her household rules—that revolving schedule of obscure prayers and masses set down during the Middle Ages, which, if faithfully observed in a state free of mortal sin, guaranteed all kinds of graces, indulgences, and divine favours after death—a quicker trip to Heaven, in other words. (Naturally, I could never understand the point of all this if you were living free of mortal sin anyhow.)

These household rules made it pretty hard to look for a job, but every time I pointed this out to my mother, she said I would have to make "sacrifices," and maybe cut an hour or two out of my sleep in order to look through all the want ads, prep my resumés and cover letters, and check the university and college calendars that offered retraining opportunities. During that time I began to see that we—Oscar and I—were both in jail, each in his own way.

By the time Oscar got out of jail and discovered where I'd been living, I was pretty much crazy, and thinking of just packing my suitcase and stepping out of Mother's place whether I had money or not, trusting in luck to provide me with another home. In fact, I was so depressed I was actually *happy* to see Oscar.

"So what the hell are you going to do?" he said, poking his head into my mother's fridge and drawing back in alarm. "I mean, you can't live *here*, can you?" He shut the door quickly and walked over to where I was sitting at the kitchen table. He was doing something weird with his hands, not wringing them but holding them out slightly in front of himself, opening and closing the fingers.

"What are *you* going to do?" I asked. He said nothing, just stood there, scratching the back of his head, an action that seemed less the result of an itch than a desire to do something with his hands. He said he had some ideas, but didn't elaborate on what those might be, and on his way out reached into his jacket for an envelope, writing a phone number on the outside where I could reach him if I wanted. Then he added, "Oh, yeah, the stuff in the envelope's for you. If you really are thinking of leaving your mother's place, then those would probably help make any decision final. On both your and your mom's part." He winked at me and stepped into the street, and that was the last time I ever saw him, moving along the sidewalk against the wind, his hands thrust so far into the front pockets of his jeans that it looked as if the pants were intent on crawling up his body and he was intent on pushing them down. Two months later, I heard he'd broken into the dead-letter office with a pair of bolt cutters but had been caught by a security guard in the midst of making his getaway, pushing a shopping cart heaped with various undeliverables, and that sometime during this pursuit he'd come to a hill, jumped into the shopping cart, and was thereby stopped, quite suddenly and fully, by a wall at the bottom. After a brief hospitalization, Oscar went back to jail.

I went up to my room with those postcards and took them out of the envelope, running my fingers along the edges of the pasted-over faces. I put them back into the envelope and tried to slip it between the mattresses of my bed, then under the newspaper at the bottom of my sock drawer, then into the vase above my television (no cable), but finally settled for wrapping the envelope in plastic, attaching a thread to one corner, and then, after several tries, lodging it in the rain gutter above my bedroom window. I let the thread hang imperceptibly along the stucco wall, within easy reach.

I have to admit there *was* something talismanic about those postcards. Whenever my mother's sanctimoniousness got to be too much, I'd lock the door to my room, reach for the string, and pull down the envelope.

My mother, for her part, suspected that because I was locking my door I was doing something bad, and she started making pornography references after a week or so, though never in direct reference to me. It was always general stuff related to the degradation and exploitation of women. (And when had she ever—during the twenty-three years I'd listened to her rant about how society would be a lot better if women stayed at home and devoted themselves to turning kids into worthwhile human beings—shown *any* sympathy for the interests of women?) Or it was pronouncements culled from various other religions (which she would have as soon seen eradicated) about how masturbation "depletes" a person, how Hinduism encouraged men to engage in sex but not to have orgasms in order to amplify and retain their "vital energies." ("Not that I'm encouraging anyone to become a Hindu," my mother said, "or not to have orgasms when having sex, since orgasms, after all, produce babies, which are wonderful in the eyes of God. All I'm saying is that one shouldn't masturbate.") She never did, however, go so far as to search my room, or, if she did, never left any sign of having done so.

Days trickled by. I spent a lot of time wandering in my mother's ornamented home, so filled with framed paintings and biblical verses that the red and golds of medieval and Byzantine art seemed to vanish into themselves, as if the sameness of the themes and motifs didn't so much transport as trap you. After a few weeks they were so pervasive they became as undifferentiated as a coat of white paint, so that I found myself wondering whether my mother had done this on purpose as a way of punishing herself, turning her home into a place of confinement, her art into a source of deprivation. My response was to run to my bedroom and get the postcards from the roof. Looking them over I smiled at the thought of what my mother would do if she caught me with them, the expression on her face identical to the one she'd wear whenever we came home from mass to find my father whistling some Bud Powell tune while loading the table with Sunday's feast.

And sometime during the weeks it took me to realize that Mother's home had been turned into its own kind of prison, I also realized the magic of the postcards: they reminded me of Father. Their profanity was a perfect realization of his own attitude toward Mother's religion, such as the time he suggested she give up going to church for Lent. The argument had some logic to it, my father proposing that it was very easy for a devout Catholic—one who truly believed that God wanted her to make various kinds of sacrifices—to give up "run-of-the-mill" things, such as eating meat, for Lent. It was no sacrifice at all, my father would continue, if at the end of the day the reward for it was eternity in the company of God. Even martyrdom, in this regard, wouldn't be enough, since it would just be trading something finite and disposable for something infinite and indispensable. No, there was only one sacrifice, as far as my father was concerned, equal to the bliss of heaven, and that was not to give up your life, but to give up your *eternal life*, to love God so much you'd even be willing to sacrifice your soul for him, for instance by not going to church anymore and damning yourself to Hell. "Now *that*," he would say, "that's a sacrifice!"

I would look at the postcards and remember his pseudo-theological arguments, and how my mother would respond by saying it wasn't for us to "presume" what kind of sacrifices God did and didn't require, and that we should have the humility to follow those practices sanctioned by Christ's representative, the Pope, and not attempt to equate our efforts with God, since it was futile to do so anyhow. For his part, he would greet her counter-argument with the same exasperation with which she greeted his, though even these discussions would end the same way Sunday brunch did, with the two of them laughing at each other and themselves.

Of course, with my father's death, everything changed. I hadn't remembered us having so many icons in the house when I was kid, and, in those first weeks of being back at my mother's, I attributed this change to the absence of my father, who wouldn't have tolerated such stifling uniformity, though I was soon to realize that it was precisely *because of my father* that Mother had turned the house into a shrine. And it had nothing to do with trying to negotiate his soul out of Purgatory.

It started with my decision to move out. She was sitting in the living room that day, listening to some interminable radio broadcast of one or more of the several messages delivered by the Pope to celebrants in St. Peter's Square, and I had to wait for forty minutes after she'd held up her finger, warning me not to interrupt. I sat there, listening to the weird delay between the Pope's Italian or Polish or Latin or whatever it was and the overlaid voice of the English translator.

"Mother, I'm moving out," I said, after she'd finally turned off the radio.

"I know," she said, shaking her hair out of her eyes. And while I was expecting her to say something else, to ask where I planned to get the money, or to question me on why her place wasn't good enough, what she ended up saying was only this: "I'm going to miss you. It's been nice having you around." But there was an edge to her regret, the feeling that I'd disappointed her, that she'd been waiting for me to do something other than sit with her through the radio broadcast, and her endless prayers, and the weekly round of masses, and I thought then, for some reason, about the postcards I'd stashed in the rain gutter, wondering if maybe the way I'd expected her to react to them was not how she would have reacted at all.

"Mother," I said. "I know you would like me to stay. But I can't spend my life keeping you company."

She looked shocked. "Is that what you think I want, for you to stay here, in this house?" She said this in a way that suggested she was thinking about what I'd just said, and, maybe for the first time in her life, conceding that there might be truths about herself she'd never considered. "Well," she said, and then waited a moment, head tilted slightly to one side, working through what I'd proposed, though when she spoke next she seemed at a total loss, for she whispered, "Really, I don't know what I was expecting. Not that, though." She looked out the window. "It was something else."

"Something what?" I asked.

"Oh," she lifted a hand to her face and then let it drop, the years of tiredness, of self-denial, of single-minded devotion coming out in her face. "I don't know." And she drew her hand, very quickly, back to her eyes. "I guess it was resistance."

I leaned forward. "Resistance? Mother, I'm moving out! Isn't that resistance enough?"

And when she looked at me next, turning back from the window, I saw her panic for the first time. "No! That's not what I meant."

"Well, what do you mean?" I was sitting there patiently, though for some reason I wanted to yell at her, demand that she start making sense. And when she said nothing I raised my voice a notch. "Listen, since I've been back here you and I have had not one single conversation. Not one! Every time I try and tell you what I want to do, what I need to be doing, you don't listen. Or you've got all your answers prepared in advance!" I wrung my hands and looked around the room. "Just once I'd like to talk to *you* rather than to some *reciter* of . . ." I waved my hands around angrily, "catechisms and truisms and . . . bullshit!"

"It's not bullshit," she said, smiling and suddenly aglow, as if my rant, rather than confronting her with our relationship, had reinforced her beliefs. "It's truth. You just don't want to face it."

"The truth?" I looked around the room, then jumped up. "The truth, Mother? All right. Hold on. I'll be back with the truth."

...

By the time I'd returned she'd put some music on, Palestrina's "The Assumption of Mary," and it was blaring at such volume I winced as I walked over to turn down the knob. Then I dropped the envelope full of postcards into her lap.

There is, of course, much that could be said about what happened next, the look in her eyes, the halting speech, the sudden spread of colour to her cheeks and forehead, and then, after that—in what now seems to me an entirely predictable event—the *laughter*, my mother shaking and shaking her head until the tears came, then rising off the couch to try and embrace me, saying I was so much like my father, so much the way he was, my mother saying it over and over and over while she shook her head and laughed.

And, oddly enough, I was less surprised at how happy she was than to find myself laughing right along with her, moving willingly into the embrace, the odd pagan moment of it all. For that is what it was, this ritual, this observance, this rite consecrated not to the salvation of our *own* souls—which is what I'd thought my mother had been doing all these years, trying to exorcise my father from the house in order to save herself—but to his memory, the two of us moving around the floor, turning circles as our laughter drowned out Palestrina. And I understood, now, that my mother's mortifications, the rigidity with which she'd lived her life since Father's death was her way of remaining faithful to him, sealing herself away from the profane until she was totally encompassed by it, held in its embrace, caressed on all sides—as if my father's spirit could be kept alive by the rigour with which she guarded against it. And her eyes shone with the look she'd worn when we would return home from mass to find my father standing in the apron with a spatula in hand, as if all her church-going, her devotions and prayers, were enacted to give him this: his moment of mockery, when he was most fully himself, the person we remembered, even now, laughing with us.

Four Uncles

THOUGH KRISZTINA wondered at my loyalties, I buried them all: Uncle Gyuri, who, having emigrated from Hungary in the early 1950s, and having watched his taxes go to social programs, insisted he'd "left one communist country only to end up in another," and who, in a fit of apoplectic rage one election night, refused to let his daughters out of the house, barring them with a shotgun because they threatened to vote for the Left; Uncle Pál, who wore scars on his back from the barbed wire he crawled under to escape a POW camp in 1946, and who, in defence of his Roman Catholicism and anti-Semitism, refuted the argument that Jesus was a Jew by saying, "Technically speaking, Christ could not be Jewish since his father was God—a non-racial entity—and his mother, Mary—a being conceived without original sin and thus not human in the classical sense either"; Uncle Ottó, who, as a boy, trapped crows for his starving family to eat during the famine that accompanied the Soviet Army into Hungary at the end of World War II, and who had no time for unemployed Quebecers and Newfoundlanders refusing to move to where the work was, saying he'd left behind not only his region and culture, but also his country, language, and family, and had arrived in Canada with nothing, working his ass off in the face of considerable obstacles to build himself a fortune, and if he could do it, then damn it they could too and with a whole lot less sacrifice and pain.

I buried them all.

...

I'd come out at the start of 1958, having spent the previous year in root cellars and attics. Friends would show up now and again, either with food, or directions to the next hiding place and the exact dates and times when I should move. Mostly, though, I was alone in places without running water, or electricity, or heat, at the mercy of shivering fears—of capture and interrogation, of being sent to a Soviet work camp—glancing between the curtains, jumping at every creak in the architecture, and reaching the point of ravening hunger before I dared go into the street, in the dead of night, to scrounge in garbage cans. Invariably, once down there, I would become so frightened of the noise I was making in my haste to find something to eat—so scared it would give me away—that I'd sprint back empty-handed to my hiding place. Within two months I'd lost fifty pounds, and was a twitchy mess.

In my solitude I began reading every book, magazine, and newspaper at hand, their content increasingly irrelevant as my situation worsened, until only words mattered, the thought that someone out there was writing against my solitude. And as minutes turned to hours and hours to days and days to weeks and weeks to months, ever more noises broke the silence of my hiding places, or, rather, what sounds there were—the ticking of walls, muffled voices from above or below, gargle of pipes—became magnified, and began to make sense, forming intelligible rhythms; until I found myself imagining that somewhere in that intelligence— both on the page and in the air—were messages from the people I'd known. And when my associates came around, once every six weeks, they'd find me eating the rot I'd scrounged on some midnight run, or drinking rainwater from the pots I dangled out the windows during thundershowers, or sitting in my room with an idiotic grin and a mass of writing spread across every surface, as though I had all the company I needed.

But when opportunity came at last—when a friend burst into the room to tell me that the time was right, that a blizzard was blanketing the western half of the country which would help me cross the border unnoticed, that there was a driver waiting to take me—there was only one person I had time for: my mother. I had kept track of her in my seclusion, relying on outside reports, in the hopes that I could bring her with me when I escaped. Things had not gone well for my mother after 1956, as they had not gone well for anyone whose immediate relatives were involved in the uprising. Denied all assistance by the state, and having no other resources, she moved in with her sister; and it was there I went that night, rushing so I would still have time to meet the driver, slipping through the heavy snows that hid me from policemen into my aunt's house, skinny as a stray dog, sneaking from room to room until I came upon the tiny broom closet where she lay in bed.

"Mother!" I hissed, leaning over her. I'll never forget it: the room so quiet you could hear snow falling beyond the open window, a clock ticking somewhere far off; and, instead of the closed eyes and sleeping face I'd expected, I saw my mother staring at me as though she'd been awake all night. And in response to my quiet cry she began to hum, and to hum, and to hum, a tune I'd never heard before. "Mother!" I hissed again. "Mother, it's me. I'm alive."

She hummed on.

And for a moment longer I stared into her eyes, thinking insane thoughts—that I might bundle her up, lead her into the blizzard, get her to ride in the truck to the border and keep quiet as we crawled past the fences and dogs and snipers. Then I gently took her hand, realizing there was no point, that she was already released, having hummed herself free of history: free of her father's death at the battle of the Don; of her mother's murder at the hands of Soviet soldiers who discovered them—her and the children— hidden in a cellar in Budapest, and who decided on a kind of R and R not at all entertaining to the children, and only entertaining to the soldiers because they'd spent two years throwing themselves in front of bullets and marching through Russian winters in boots flapping at the soles; free of her three brothers' disappearance into

fates she obsessed about, bolting up in bed or in the middle of lac-
ing her shoes, as one tormented by waking nightmares; and, finally,
of the apparent deaths of her husband and her one and only son,
who'd both been too active in the cause of 1956.

I do not remember how I felt, sitting by her bed that night,
though I recall consoling myself with the thought that she was
beyond loss; for she said nothing as I described how I'd passed the
year since the uprising—how afraid I'd been to compromise her by
making contact (even to say I was alive), why I was running, and
from whom, and what would happen if they caught me—because
she seemed not to be listening, neither replying nor glancing in my
direction nor hardly breathing.

Instead, she simply looked around the room as if its walls formed
the limits of her world, beyond which there was nothing to speak or
hear of. It was as if the year I'd spent in similar confines
demanded—in an inverted logic—another person, my mother, to
be driven crazy for reasons opposite to those that had nearly claimed
my sanity: the sight of all that space—trees and lakes and mountains
and sky and whole nations—into which her family had vanished;
the proximity of people in the cities she'd searched, crowds upon
crowds upon crowds, everyone in the world but the one she desperately wanted to see; all that language forced into her ears and eyes by
people who demanded dialogue: the local workers council who
expelled her from her job for having "harboured" (that is, given
birth to) a counter-revolutionary; neighbours who scolded her for
raising a son of dubious character; policemen who'd come by, day
after day, demanding she tell them who my "friends" were; and,
finally, the only person she could rely upon, her older sister, who
took her in but spent the days disguising her anxiety with long sighs.
All those noises except the few words she needed to hear. Until it was
not so much what she'd lost that my mother battled against, but the
sense of loss itself, a battle she could only win—or so my aunt told
me later that night, handing me a bag of clothes and food for the
journey—by turning from the agents who followed wherever she

went (in the hopes that she'd lead them to others like me); twisting away from the mailbox (word never arrived) toward a small room at the back of the house where she made her bed one night; by avoiding all language that was either a response or which required one, and humming, instead, quiet songs in a place so little, *so already a prison*, that no one could ever take it away.

I have added her—my mother as she was on the night I last saw her—to my teetering tower of guilt, though even after all this (indeed, perhaps because of it) I am not sure she still wouldn't have wanted me to fight, to take part in the suicide that was our October of 1956. I do not know whether my escape from Hungary was enough—*finally enough*—to kill her, but I too wake at night, bent on the sheets, imagining that room she chose for herself, to which the price of entry was dereliction of self, a dropping of everything that defined you like a worn coat in the doorway.

You would not believe the network of refugees they had in the 1950s. You could head over to the Arany Tyúk in Toronto and mention to a waitress the name of some relative you'd last seen in 1944, and whom you thought may have come to Canada, though perhaps Australia, and within months she'd introduce you to some old guy in a leather hunting cap (which made him the laughing-stock of everyone on the street), who'd tell you he'd shared a shack in an Austrian refugee camp with your long-lost relative, and had recently received a postcard from Vancouver with his signature at the bottom. In those days, we specialized in everything, including coincidence.

So by 1965, a short seven years after my escape, I had made contact with all three of my uncles.

Gyuri died first, on a bitter February day when he realized that, despite the corruption everywhere evident in the Liberal government, the Conservatives were not going to win the next election. I was there a few days before he died—along with his émigré wife and three daughters—when Gyuri rose from the sickbed and pointed emphatically at the mantelpiece, continuing to rise and grunt and point, wasting his remaining strength, until they brought everything on it down to him: a vase, a picture of himself as a young soldier, a ring that had belonged to my grandmother, and, finally, the item that calmed him—an envelope containing his official membership in the Conservative party. He died holding that paper to his heart.

And here's where my troubles began. Krisztina, Gyuri's eldest daughter, only five years younger than I, recalled to me our family tradition, which I knew little about, having left Hungary before being fully introduced to ancestral lore. It was she who came to visit me a few days after we'd sat around Gyuri's bedside, watching the respirator rise and fall.

She was carrying a letter, old and creased from having been folded and refolded, as though the sender had been unsure of the writing he'd placed upon it, or to whom it should be addressed. It was Gyuri's will. "In accordance with the tradition of the Kassai family, I would like my remains to be buried by my nearest male blood relatives." Frowning, Krisztina fanned the letter in my face. "That's you," she said.

I looked at the clumsy handwriting, the left-out or misplaced accents, the interruption of the flow of Hungarian by the occasional English word conjugated to fit, and then gazed at Krisztina with an expression that indicated how far we'd come from Hungary (she and her sisters had never even been there!), as well as the obligation I felt to the history we'd suffered through. "You know," she said quietly, looking at me, "I thought you would be happy to ignore this." She glanced at the letter as if she wished she'd never brought it to my attention. "I loved my father," she continued, the softness of her tone edged with a bitterness verging on hostility, "but I can't say I liked him. He never had time to listen to us. We were women. Pegged us even before we were born. And, you know, that's the main thing he instilled into us: loyalty to principles first, loyalty to people second." Krisztina laughed humourlessly, "I wonder what he'd think if he knew that *my principles* say we—my sisters and I—should be the ones to bury him. And *him* and *his wishes* can come second." She looked at me and smiled then, putting the heel of one hand up to her eyes. "Why weren't we good enough to bury him? Can't women hold shovels as good as anybody?"

I looked at the paper, recalling how Gyuri had treated his daughters, a bear of a man, stained sweaters and emphysema, the way he could slam a door or stare at the boyfriends they brought home, standing at the kitchen table glaring at them as though they were strangers come into the house uninvited, utterly silent, before finally asking, "Are you Hungarian? Are you, at least, German?" They never were; and when his youngest, Gyöngyi, took up with a foreign exchange student from China, Gyuri once again went into the envelope I was holding, and made another of his thousand emendations.

"A Chinaman!" roared Gyuri (in Hungarian, of course) that day in the office of the transmission repair shop I'd managed to scrape out of the earth and pile up on a corner of Kingsway. "I've always told my daughters! Always!" he continued, "One of the beautiful things about this world is all the different races in it. A wonder— all these races!" he shook his finger at me. "And we have a duty and responsibility to keep it that way!"

While he was staring out the window in a rage, I reached forward carefully and plucked from his grasp the wedding invitation sent by Gyöngyi and her fiancé.

I tried very hard not to think badly of Gyuri then, watching the stillness of the fingers I'd taken the invitation from, quivering as though they'd lost their grip on something, though he refused to believe it, thinking this something just beyond reach, as if the right strings were dangling just millimetres above, though of course he gave himself reason upon reason for not reaching up, since he did not want to risk the fact that everything that had defined his life—that he *still* defined it by—was not only out of range but out of existence.

I waited in a chair, the smell of carbolic on my hands, trying to find some way to present my thoughts in the form of praise, though in truth I had little to say, wanting only to point out that by turning his daughters into mementoes of the country he'd left he'd also turned them into reminders of the consequences of leaving, so that every time he looked at them, they rubbed his nose into a soil he'd risked life and limb for them to walk upon. And while he prided himself on this, he had never once, really, touched down on Canadian earth, moving along as if he were somehow insulated from it by the layer of Hungarian dust he'd been so careful not to kick from his heels. It was, perhaps, time for him to look down.

And, in the end, this bit of equivocation, this "perhaps," was the only concession I could make to Gyuri, and he reacted to it exactly as expected, turning from the window to shout that he had escaped Hungary, he really had, and I was a *seggfej* for suggesting he hadn't. Moreover, he was more than "man enough" to take Canada on its own terms.

Within months, Gyöngyi and Li Peng were married at the Vancouver Hungarian Cultural Centre, the whole thing paid for by Gyuri, who walked among the milling crowds of confused Asians and Hungarians as a holy man might along a path of nails, the difference being that Gyuri's coolness was the result of such self-control it was not coolness at all but rather a kind of psychological fascism. For if holy men transcend the self, achieving a plane above, Gyuri had liquidated it, and was thus nowhere. He walked as if his insides had gone dead and grey, and when I followed him into the alley outside the hall I found him leaning against a wall and weeping; and he, turning to see me, said, "I have escaped! I have!" and waved me back inside.

Krisztina and Cili had it easier than Gyöngyi, but since neither of them married a Hungarian or German, Gyuri was not much more natural at their ceremonies either, especially after learning that Jason, Krisztina's fiancé, had distant Jewish blood, and that Ed, Cili's husband, belonged to a family with historical connections to the labour movement. The only thing worse than being of the wrong race was being of the wrong political persuasion.

The three daughters, of course, had little admiration for Gyuri's discipline. They saw only the beads of sweat on his face, the fingers digging at his armpits, the utter lack of grace, and resented him for never being able to relax around their husbands and kids (his own grandchildren!), whom he patted as if there were handprints telling him exactly where to place his palm and fingers. Unlike me, the three daughters had never had Gyuri's image before their eyes, guiding them when everything else was lost; and I was incapable of explaining to them the connection between this image and the bully who'd raised them.

By the time I buried Gyuri, Pál and Ottó were geriatrics, the former leaning on two canes, the latter with a private nurse to hold up his IV pole. I saw them from where I stood, both men having to be forcibly restrained (which wasn't too difficult, given their infirmities) from grabbing and wielding one of the shovels struck into the dirt by the grave. Gyuri, being naturally lazy, was easy to dissuade, but Ottó was a different case, and his language became ever more colourful as he tried to shake off the nurse and me—cursing up and down about how he was a "free man," how he'd overcome physical extremes "far worse" than old age and heart disease and encroaching mortality, and how "by Christ" there wasn't a man alive, "not one," with the strength to prevent him "doing right by family tradition"—in a tug-of-war that went on for twenty minutes before Krisztina finally had to step forth, lay a gentle hand on the old man's tailored sleeve, and stare him down. The intensity of her tear-stained eyes forced him to relinquish the shovel and gaze at the ground in shame.

And so, as I dug, and despite how obviously infirm Pál and Ottó were, I couldn't help but see two men whose escapes, by the summer of 1954—because we had no information, because their letters could not get to us, because no one who'd seen them go had returned to tell of it—had become legendary. The two men looked so faint on the afternoon I buried Gyuri—their outlines chalk traces upon the day—that it made me thankful I was so young at the time of my escape, not because it meant I was healthy, but because of youth's idealism and its accompanying amnesia, because if I'd really known what my uncles were like they would not have been there to guide my steps. For if history is determined by the quality of the explanations we offer for events, then the luck of youth is not to inquire too deeply into that quality, even when it carves its saints out of reactionaries. But perhaps I am only making excuses, because even later, once their characters came clear, I always tried to support them. And I suppose if this story is anything then it is the confession of an accessory who, while recognizing his sin, continued to help the men with whom he's been condemned.

Because they lost their lives. I'm not speaking biologically, of course, but I knew, even in the autumn of 1956, that to stay in Hungary and die was not to fight as they had, as only a single person *can* fight: by leaving. Theirs was the type of battle where you are always a casualty, a battle in which—rather than watering your country with your blood, making it fertile through martyrdom—you leave it worse for your absence. This was their paradox: that, when they left, they did not go for reasons of a better life elsewhere, but because dissent demanded it, because they wanted to strike some kind of blow, even while knowing that exile was a relinquishing, not only of a country but also of the only life that mattered. It was this I thought of, often, in the year following 1956, when the things that had once provided warmth—my country, my village, my home, my people—lost all worth the second I went into hiding, the second I could no longer share them with anyone; so that no matter how I concentrated, struggling to remember every detail, they were as little use to me as a secret that cannot be told, a love letter without a recipient.

Uncle Pál, like Uncle Ottó, did not have any children. He loved keeping tin goods unopened, stacked in tall columns in the kitchen, until whatever was inside began to rot, expelling gasses that bent the tops and bottoms of the cans convex, making them even more precious to Pál, who hoarded them in the absence of all usefulness, treasuring them though their contents were spoiled, inedible, a testament to a hunger so great you'll stack rot against the fear of experiencing it again. As I learned after Pál died, he spent most of his life writing for right-wing periodicals published by Orthodox Catholics, radical Hungarians, and other fascist nostalgics in Australia, who sent him money to supplement his UI and welfare cheques, and (when things got bad) the money I gave him for helping sort nuts and bolts, steam clean engines, and—when he didn't find it too demeaning—make coffee and stroll down Kingsway to pick up lunch for my mechanics.

Pál often spoke about having children, lamenting not his own failure in this regard but mine. "You need to get yourself a wife," he'd say. "A Catholic. One who'll go around and clap your kids' hands together to pray." And on those nights when I was unable to sleep, I would move around my apartment and look down at my slack, skinny belly (loss of appetite was only one legacy of my time in hiding), pacing in circles, thinking how little difference there was between Pál and me, both of us so afraid of bringing children into the world we were awkward in the company of women, flinching involuntarily from images of suffering, whether in magazines, or on TV, or in our imaginations, as if what we'd endured made us incapable of considering anyone else—much less a child—having to face even a tenth of it. We'd lost our faith not only in humanity but also in the process of being human, though I hope that I, at least, was not stuck in a holding pattern, hanging onto the days until one finally came along that defied my grip. And on these sleepless nights I knew I could call him, no matter how late, that he would be up when no one else was, and that while the conversation would be stilted and halting there was at least something to listen to other than the ticking of the clock and the relentless churn of memory.

We had quiet arguments whenever he came to the garage. During these, my responses were always silent. He'd make a remark about the shape of one of the mechanic's noses, or about some customer who'd tried to shortchange us, and I would simply stare at him, or off to one side, leaving him unsure of whether my unresponsiveness was agreement or dissent. Afterwards, he'd disappear for a few days, though he always came back, saying he needed the money.

I remember Krisztina coming to see me the night after the police entered Pál's apartment. He'd passed away days earlier in the solitude of his home, meaning that his body had begun stinking up the corridor between suites before anyone noticed. "The police came to see me," she said. "They had a boxful of books and papers. You should have seen this stuff!" She shook her head. I didn't ask Krisztina what Pál's writing was about because I already knew, thinking back to those nights when we'd spoken on the telephone, back to the things he'd admitted, both of us speaking through the fevers of insomnia. "The policeman wanted to launch an investigation, but there didn't seem to be any collaborators."

"He didn't have anyone," I said, answering a different question.

"You know that he made me and my sisters his principal beneficiaries? We don't want any of that money!"

"He didn't have any money," I said.

"Are you kidding?" Krisztina replied, pulling out a file prepared
by the lawyer for Pál's estate. "He had it squirrelled away everywhere!" I held the bank books, squinting down the neat columns
of deposits, which Pál apparently made on regular dates, times
when he'd come begging to me for work, and during which he'd
received the money I'd given him (he insisted on being paid in
cash) in cupped hands, as if receiving the Eucharist. But where had
the rest come from? (Surely, hate literature didn't sell *that* well?)

"I've spoken to Cili and Gyöngyi. None of us wants the money.
There are organizations. Jewish museums. Holocaust education.
We could donate it. . . ."

"That would be a good idea," I said, quietly.

"You're not . . ." Krisztina looked out the window. "I mean you
wouldn't contest it if we did that . . . ?"

I turned my eyes to her, stunned. "You think I would mind?" I
couldn't help it, I was shouting. "I knew he hated Jews, but I didn't
know he wrote that—" I waved my hand at her, though she wasn't
holding anything other than the file, "—that garbage!"

"Well." Krisztina smiled carefully, neither out of amusement nor
happiness, but rather in defence of my aggression. "I know you
were close to Pál bácsi, and I thought maybe . . ."

"You think I was sympathetic to that?"

Krisztina looked at the ground. "My father spoke highly of you. I
can't see him doing that unless the person he spoke about was like
him. . . . He and Pál bácsi got along, you know."

I opened my mouth to yell some more, then closed it, at a loss as
to how to justify myself to Krisztina, to explain my devotion to her
father, to Pál, to Ottó, without at the same time implicating myself
in their insanity. Anyhow, I couldn't be sure I *wasn't* implicated,
since the trauma that had warped and ossified their thinking, that

had made of them brutal and twitchy obsessive-compulsives, was also *my* trauma, though I would have liked to think I was not a fascist, and that Krisztina and her sisters knew it. And yet, how else could I explain an affection for the three men that was prepared to overlook almost anything (though that was wrong, too, for I certainly would not have given money to Pál had I known of his stash, nor tolerated the publication of his anti-Semitic rants)? Instead, I asked, "Did your father really hurt you that badly?"

"I didn't have much of a father," said Krisztina, after a moment of silence. "He was never really here. I think history ended for him the moment he left Hungary. I don't know what kind of truths they had then, but it seemed like he held on to them long after they'd become the worst kind of lies."

And to that, really, there was no response.

The priest and I buried Pál. I suppose Father Conklin pitied me that overcast day, grabbing an extra shovel the minute he'd finished with the service, the two of us working in silence as a warm wind blew in from offshore, carrying a spring rain so gentle it felt as if we were passing through spiders' webs. There was nobody else willing to come to the funeral, not even Ottó, who claimed to be too sick, though I knew for a fact that Pál had disgusted him, and that, for Ottó, Gyuri's funeral had been a happy occasion, since it was the last time he would ever have to see Pál again or acknowledge their relation. On hearing I was burying Pál, he'd said, "I hope he left you something in return!" Well, he *has* left me something, I thought at the time, though both Ottó and I knew that neither Gyuri nor Pál (nor Ottó himself, for that matter) were inclined to financially reward the duties of tradition.

It took the priest and me twenty minutes to pile all the dirt on Pál's casket, and maybe another five for the priest to utter a few parting remarks.

And then it was over, an entire life done with, and not a soul except me to acknowledge or weigh it against Krisztina's condemnation, which, it seemed to me, was relevant not because it addressed Gyuri and Pál's failure to escape the truths of their times—to acknowledge the contradiction between its Christianity and hate—since, let's face it, very few are capable of this, but because it addressed their failure—both of them having outlived those times—to gaze back in recognition, and use the remorse that gaze *should have* occasioned against the illusions that comforted and rotted them for the rest of their lives.

Upon leaving the cemetery I thought I saw Krisztina's car moving off the avenue that led from the cemetery to the freeway, but there are too many red cars in the world for me to be sure, and it was probably just an illusion of my own, a hope that Krisztina's presence at the funeral in some way signified an awareness of the failure, this time mine, that demanded I be present at Pál's funeral.

But if she was there, she never mentioned it.

Of all my uncles, Ottó's was the only death at which I was actually present. Unlike Gyuri—whom he liked but didn't have a lot in common with—or Pál—whom he hated—Ottó had never seen me as a confidant, never come to me in moments of familial or financial crisis, though we met often enough, sitting on his back verandah and telling jokes, talking politics, reminiscing, our brains awash in more than a few shots of pear brandy. Our relationship consisted of maintaining the distance required by politeness, like waltzing partners determined to keep a full twelve inches between their bodies, so that when one of us moved forward (metaphorically of course, say by asking a personal question), the other would move back (answering with another question, or with an impersonal reference, bringing up a historical or political reason for why they had broken off with this or that woman). Ottó always wore a suit, often of linen, and his shirts were crisply pressed, his style so impeccable that it dominated his personality and made it impossible to think of either Gyuri or Pál as his siblings. Ottó was a member of not just the local Hungarian club, but was a "friend" (financial contributor) to the Vancouver Symphony, as well as a host of other cultural institutions. He was the sort of man who received invitations to formal functions, and nods in the hallways when business took him to city hall.

"You know," he said as I sat by his bed the night he died, "Pál was an idiot. Really! I shouldn't talk about him that way," he interrupted his confession with an extended period of wheezing, and I saw the fear in his eyes afterwards, as if—for reasons of death, and whatever might lie beyond it—he was considering not making fun of his brother, though a second later he shrugged and continued, "but what else can you say about a man who smokes two packs a day, doesn't exercise, eats mouthfuls of lard, and then tells you, because he doesn't like to bathe, that a lot of our health problems today can be traced to the fact that our society showers too much? 'Washing away all of our natural oils,' he'd say! 'That's why we're all so sick and allergic to everything.' You know what my response was? 'You stink!' That's what I'd say. 'You stink!' And he'd reply, 'It's a manly smell.' A manly smell! Can you believe it?" Ottó shook his head, smiling at the memory.

"And then there was Gyuri," he grimaced. "Pig-headed, that's what! You could have used his skull to hammer nails! I can't believe that his daughters didn't poison him." He began laughing now, as the pain of the cancer and the euphoria of morphine confused his responses. "Maybe they did, maybe they did," he said, growing thoughtful and quiet, and taking his eyes from mine to let them wander in sudden fits and starts along the pictures mounted on the walls, the collection of leather-bound books on the mantelpiece, as if whatever he was looking at wavered before him; and when he spoke next it was exclusively to these flitting spirits.

"Stop it! Both of you," Ottó shouted. "You—neither of you!—don't know what it was like. You only complained." Ottó's voice faltered now, and when he spoke again it was lower than a whisper. "You only knew what it was like to wake up with teeth inside your stomach. Staring at the dark. You knew the coldness of the room but not what it was like to step into those boots. It was like putting your feet into blocks of ice. Then out, while it was still night. Along the fences, under them, every step in fear of unexploded shells. I was only twelve years old! And what kept me moving were those teeth, gnawing upwards from my stomach, burning in my throat. Twelve years old: the oldest boy, but smaller than a man. Under the fences, in the fields. Sometimes hiding for hours beneath a bridge, in empty pigpens and henhouses, anywhere the Russians might not look. With Grandfather's watch in my pocket—something to give them if they caught me. My fingers so stiff with cold I was afraid to bend them.

"Then to the traps, the crows, some already frozen, some feeble, gone the whole night squawking, flapping their wings, losing heat. One twist of the neck with my child's hands, then into the bag. Baiting the traps again. And then back home after being out in that winter—why was it so cold then?—sometimes four hours, back home, on a good day, with one, maybe two, standing in the kitchen with my hands in my armpits, trembling with cold. I had to pluck the birds. Mother refused to. Refused to kiss me until I put my cold hands in the cold water to wash them.

"And then the two of you and father at the table. Mother ladling out the soup. The smallest amount of grease on its surface. Twig-like bones coming to the surface. Wrinkling your noses, eating only out of the most desperate hunger, pausing to catch your breath between each spoonful, looking at me accusingly. 'Couldn't you catch a sparrow?' father said. 'There are better birds out there than crows.' 'A crow belongs to the songbird family,' mother always replied.

"It tasted like shit. That's what crows ate in those days. The shit in the fields, the manure, the bugs, rotting leaves falling from the trees, the mud packed up on the sides of the ditches along the road, crumbs of bread fallen between the prints left by the soles of marching soldiers, rotted meat of fallen horses, broken eggshells on the floors of chicken coops, the grubs and offal from where the slaughter went on, both in the yards and elsewhere, out there, in the forest, where the Germans had marched those people from our village, out there from where the ringing shots could be heard, one volley, a pause, then another, wave upon wave, out there in the forest where we were forbidden to go—the crows eating it all up, whatever could be scavenged, whatever fit inside their beaks, until it was like they'd swallowed everything, from the dirt to the blood, until the crows seemed composed of the earth under the frost and snow and slush and our feet—composed of the country itself— bits and pieces torn away from the ground, flung up into the sky to land in my traps.

"That's what we ate. And you complained and complained and complained, forcing it down past the tightening in your throat. Mother spoke of songbirds."

And now, Ottó, in a spasm, forced his eyes away from the patterns they were weaving upon, or seeing within, the air; and with a supreme effort—as if by sheer will he could push himself one last time between the walls of pain that separated us—met my eyes with such intensity, I felt as though it would throw me from my chair.

"And how many times," he said, his voice almost at a conversational level, "how many times, in all the thirty years since, would we have murdered for that taste, killed for it—betrayed everything for just one more bite?"

And with that he closed his eyes and died.

Krisztina, Cili, and Gyöngyi came to Ottó's funeral, along with half the city. It was disconcerting to stand before what was easily five hundred people, most of whom were extremely uncomfortable watching me work the shovel alone, and would have gladly joined in had Ottó's strictly worded testament permitted it. But I dug the shovel in, dropping dirt on the casket, until it was over, the crowd waiting patiently for me to finish, at which point they came and shook my hand, some of whom—not realizing I was Ottó's blood relation—even stuffing money into my pockets.

The three women and I were strangers in the reception hall, where it seemed everyone but us knew everyone else, as if the businessmen and politicians, lawyers and accountants, and members of private clubs were Ottó's true family, and the three girls and me only hired help.

"I wonder if any of these people knew who Ottó's brothers were?" asked Krisztina, punching her fork into the roast beef.

I picked at the potato salad, thinking of the soup Ottó had described, before pushing my plate away. I sat for a minute more, watching the girls eat, then rose abruptly—a man jerked up, something biting at his spine—and staggered outside into the parking lot, where I wandered in a daze, back and forth between the bumpers and fenders, my jacket catching on side-view mirrors, my pants rubbing on dirty tires, feeling as if there were something out here, a place I might get to where I could alleviate this sense of loss; though there was only the endless parking lot, in which—no matter how I moved, left or right—I came no nearer to the perimeter, as if the cars had been parked there to perpetuate a maze without exit.

By the time Krisztina found me, I was nearly in tears with desperation, and she folded her arms around me, whispering, "You really loved those old men." And though her tone and touch expressed sympathy, it was entirely without understanding, done out of love for the griever rather than in recognition of the grief, a comfort no different from what you might give a child on the death of a goldfish.

And how would I have explained it to her, had I lifted my head and managed to get the words out? "They were afraid—" I might have said, "—afraid all their lives." But I was not looking to excuse them, to chart their offences as if every step had been decided by what they'd survived, as if those horrors determined, for the rest of their lives, what they would never again willingly face. For there is nothing like trauma to make one rage for certainty, to make one invest one's belief in the ugliest of securities—fascism and greed—and to mistake the form this belief takes for reality, when the truth is you are too frightened, too demoralized, to cope with a world that does not accommodate faith. Thinking back now, I know this is what I should have said, not on behalf of those three men—they were too far gone to be helped—but on behalf of those who had lived with them, who had spent all those years trying to get them to negotiate the terms of a relationship, when any form of negotiation—and the compromise it entailed—would have forced them back to a world they could not abide, far from that nowhere untouched by change or violence or unpredictability that they'd invented to make the running easier. Their principal mistake was thinking they were in exile when they'd always been home.

But, in truth, the only thing that occurred to me, the only images that came to mind, the only words I might have articulated, were exactly the ones Krisztina would not have understood. Her anger, and her suffering under Gyuri, were too strong for her to comprehend my debt to these three men. Or, rather, she would have understood, but without experiencing, what it was like to wait weeks and weeks in absolute silence, listening to the ticking of a house and the rumbling of your stomach; rationing your remaining food in ever tinier portions, halving and halving and halving what remains until you seem to be splitting atoms; wondering who will deliver the next knock at the door: the man with the fresh bread and safe addresses, or the guards too happy to hammer your fingers from the table leg as they drag you away; and, finally, risking capture to make one last visit to your mother, to the one person not defaced by absence and isolation, only to realize she said goodbye to you a lifetime ago, and because she is no longer part of this world, neither are you, having lost so much in those tiny rooms that flight is not a risk but an admission that you've survived all you care to survive, stumbling by night through the driving snow, having said goodbye, crawling west across an almost unprotected stretch of border knowing that even before the first step you have already gone much farther than you wanted, along a journey from which none of us returned.

Because the tragedy was this: during that winter trek, there was only one light strong enough to blot out the memory of my mother—or strong enough to redeem what had happened to her, to my father, to me—and it was the faces of my uncles glimmering through the snow and trees in defiance of the distance ahead and the greater distance behind, assuring me that certain acts of resistance require you to run not to save your life but to lose it, and in losing add another corpse to the dead piled on the doorstep of those responsible. I was, in a sense, joining them and my mother in the only form of dissent left us. And I realized then that what I had been looking for in the parking lot—and even from Krisztina—was forgiveness, when the only thing I had any right to truly expect was condemnation. For if in the moment of defeat I had been drawn to my uncles as to a light, then it was my failure, and crime, that nothing they did or said after that terrible winter of 1958 had ever really been able to diminish it.

Into the Ring

MY WIFE AND I are watching that scene in *Snatch* where Brad Pitt, after being battered to no effect by some enormous boxer, finally steps to the side as his opponent charges and cracks him one on the jaw, sending him down to the floor and into a head-brace for the remainder of the movie. My wife turns to me at this point and says, somewhat incredulously, "They don't expect us, *I mean seriously*, to believe that a little guy like Brad could take out a bruiser that size with only *one punch?*"

This is something of a challenge to me—for I am a "little guy"—so I tell her about Floyd Nolan, a sort-of friend I had in high school who one drunken night smoked Lenny Robinson, a towering scrum-prop, with an uppercut that knocked him out for three minutes. "Floyd was only five foot nine," I say, "and maybe one hundred and sixty pounds, while Lenny was something like six foot four and well over two twenty." The trick was that Floyd knew how to hit, having trained as a youngster with some guy whose first name nobody ever figured out, but who was called "Bum" Bourdieu, and who ran a boxing clinic for elementary school kids in the basement of the United Church every Sunday afternoon after Bible class.

"Okay, I'll prove it to you again. Get the gloves," she says.

And here we go.

My wife—whose name is Smolinka Kafelnikov (mine is William Foresmith)—is anything but a "little guy." And I suspect the reason she's so bothered by the scene in *Snatch*, and my anecdote about Floyd and Lenny, is because she identifies with the bruisers of the world, and thinks it's obscene the way they always end up on the mat, KO'd by some pretty-boy who in real life can't take two steps out of Hollywood without this squad of massive body-guards. "They're selling the myth of the little man," she says. "As if all you need to get anywhere in this world is a little bit of spunk and the right expertise. If that's so, then how come these stars are always surrounded by guys built like brick shithouses? How come they're never surrounded by a bunch of Jackie Chans?" My wife believes that everyone, especially the pretty-boys, knows that 250 pounds of muscle is a lot harder to get through than 170, and Ali beating Foreman back in 1974 just proves the rule—because it *was* an upset, because the sportscasters *were* amazed that the smaller, weaker Muhammad managed to pull off the victory. But this, and any other historical counter-example I might bring up, is just an opportunity for Smolinka to prove how right she is—with her fists.

We haven't put on the gloves in maybe six months, not since the business went under, and it seems a shame to spoil our evenly tied record at this late a date (actually, as she's quick to point out, the record is not so evenly tied, since, yes, we've each got a total of twenty-five victories, but only eight of mine are knockouts, the rest points, while a full twenty of hers ended with me toppling to the floor—twice with a concussion).

Today she doesn't even wait for me to get the gloves on, but rabbit punches me in the back of the head as I'm trying to get my hands into them. She always was a cheater. And a ref baiter. Smolinka was one of those girls who outperformed the boys. She was a long- and high-jumper, a sprinter, a marathon ace, a swimmer, a soccer player, and a home-run hitter—one of those all-around athletes who's actually been careful to keep up her high school muscle tone. Of course, she was never very good at anything that required finesse, at pitching or tennis or target shooting—and that's where I sometimes have an edge on her in the ring, moving side to side, up and down, showing her that power means nothing if you can't make it connect.

And these days, what with her being eight months pregnant, it's easier than ever to outmanoeuvre Smolinka. On the other hand, she does have a hell of a lot more weight behind each fist, meaning that if I get distracted, or duck to the wrong side just once, and she connects, I might find myself steering straight for the mat, guided by that constellation of stars known only to victims of concussion and whiplash. So it's bob and weave, bob and weave, while she pants and grunts and curses her reduced lung capacity. I bounce out of the corners and try sticking to the edges of the ring, where there's less light, where it's harder for her to tell the difference between my shadow and me. Naturally, I'm as handicapped as she is, since the only place I *should* be hitting her is between the forehead and the neck, while she's got me from the belly up.

I was never much of a talent at sports. Oh sure, I was average. I played on the teams and got my share of assists and goals. I suppose the best you could say was that I was reliable, a good seventh or eighth pick, not somebody who'd make a difference to winning or losing, but who could provide just the right kind of backup so that the star forwards would have a chance to shine. And so I was a little more leery than Smolinka when the marriage counsellor suggested boxing as a kind of coping mechanism for two people trapped in a failing relationship.

But it worked. For years we'd been trying to get pregnant. We went to fertility clinics and impregnation conferences and psychic procreation workshops and even to some guy who recommended winding a certain kind of sea kelp around my dick during intercourse. Nothing worked. And Smolinka was so upset, I think, because her body, or what she wanted to do with it, had never been an obstacle before. Suddenly it was as if the laws of physics had bitten her on the ass, awakening her to the fact that there were limits to what she could attain. So she had plenty of rage to channel into jabs and uppercuts and haymakers. *Plenty.*

We were sitting in the kitchen the day we discovered that our inability to bear children was "negatively impacting" our marriage. Smolinka was making smoothies, I remember, with bananas, milk, blueberries, and apple, and I was leafing through some obscure nineteenth-century manual (yes, we were that desperate) on the merits of Dr. Kolfass's "East Indies remedy for the barren marriage," whose recipe involved various kinds of dung beetles, when I just slammed the book shut and said, "You know, maybe we should adopt." That's when Smolinka whipped around, ripped the blender lid off and doused me with smoothie. "Oh, sure," she yelled, "that's just like you, isn't it? Encounter one tiny problem and then, wham, just give up without trying." I sat there with banana and blueberries dripping off my head, thinking to myself, *without trying?* Here I was, poring over a recipe developed by some snake-oil salesman, and thinking seriously, *seriously,* about giving it a go, after having spent months and years and thousands of dollars on medical procedures and hypnotists and all manner of touchy-feely therapy, and she's accusing me of not trying? "Listen, I know this has been hard for you, Smolinka; it's been hard for me, too. But, you know, you can't walk on water, for Christ's sake, and if we can't have kids we just can't have kids!"

"That's the problem with you, William—you just don't have an athlete's attitude! You just don't have the will to win! I don't know if I can be married to someone like that."

Well, she was right about one thing.

And the marriage counsellor went on at some length about my "attitude" before he decided that we needed to get into the ring.

Smolinka circles around me now, her every step working to force me into a corner, to cut off my room to manoeuvre, but I'm still ducking the punches, moving away under her arms as they swing into empty air above my head. She hasn't learned to compensate for the huge weight that's developed around her waist over the last few months, and each shot sends her off balance, though not so off that I can connect with more than a light tap to the side of her head. I weave out, surprised at how much boxing strategy she's retained, though I can feel a certain amount of it coming back as well. It's just that I'm sweating, and she's not even breathing hard—not even with the pregnancy.

We started off taking lessons, on the counsellor's recommendation. Smolinka, as I said, was a natural, picking up the moves and rhythms almost effortlessly, while I usually had to put in an extra day of practice—often on the sly—just to stay on the learning curve. This went on for months, and the marriage did seem to improve, at least in the sense that we were both too tired to go at one another, especially late into the night as we'd been used to doing.

By the time we started sparring, Smolinka and I were both a little obsessed. I was reading boxing history, tons of it, and poring over videotapes of matches, from the earliest to the latest, which you could order by the crate from a place called Boxingenthusi-asts.com. Smolinka, on the other hand, was just going at the bag, night after night, working on that hard, incredible, killer punch that only needed to connect once. So while I was getting "scientific," she was getting deadly. There were no quote marks around anything that woman did.

The very first time we stepped into the ring she gave me my first concussion. They tell you you see stars, and since the invention of the comics this has become the cliché of the big hit, that or birds swirling around your head, but the iconography is dead on, and I went off into deep space that first time, drifting farther and farther toward the mat as time slowed to molasses and I sank in it, knowing that there was no way I could move fast enough to stop what was happening—despite the slow motion of everything else around me. They used smelling salts to bring me back.

After that I got smart, and she only gave me one more concussion. I even got to love boxing, although studying the moves of the pros, and making sure my technique never fell into a pattern Smolinka could predict, was as much a survival tactic as a passion.

This went on for a year, things moving along just fine, except for those nights when I pulled off a victory or, worse, actually managed to knock her out (which I could only do via the "rope-a-dope" tactic, preserving my innards and face while Smolinka, impatient as ever, bounced shots off my forearms and fists until she was nearly falling over with fatigue, at which point I'd step in and clock her one with a short, stiff punch). On nights like that we wouldn't really talk much, Smolinka turning up the radio really loud on the car ride home.

As the boxing took over our lives we stopped talking about kids. By now, we'd converted part of the basement into an okay-sized workout area and built an extension off the back carport to house the ring we'd bought as a joint Christmas present. It was as if we were channelling all our grievances into the sport, with the effect that we had something constructive to talk about, a hobby we could work at together, and which left us, as I said, too tired from the workouts, or too focused on the next bout, to really have room for anything else.

That's when we made a mistake.

At present, my mistake is not having tied double knots in my laces. And while I'm looking down and wondering how I'm going to tie them without taking off my gloves or, more important, dropping my guard, Smolinka raises my chin with a startling uppercut. My head snaps back and blackness floods my vision. She hammers three punches into my rib cage and I fall against the rope, breathing heavy. And when I try and twist on the ropes, I step on the damn lace and go farther off balance, so that she smacks me on either ear, one two, one two, a couple of times. The automatic bell rings just as she's winding up, and I fall to my knees, narrowly escaping a knockout. "My shoelaces became untied," I say. She shrugs, bouncing around the ring to her corner, leaving me in a squat, marvelling at how muscular her legs are, without a trace of cellulite, even with an eight-month fetus on the make. And I wonder why I'm calling it a "fetus" all of sudden, depersonalizing it, when it's always just been the "baby." Why this sudden rage, just when I thought I'd put all those feelings behind me? I crawl to my corner, pull off my gloves, and tie my shoelace, wiping blood from my nose onto a towel hanging from the corner.

The problem was that the boxing, instead of decreasing Smolinka's anger toward me, only seemed to fuel it. Oh sure, we didn't argue anymore, and I didn't find myself covered in smoothie or red wine or dishwashing water, but she had this ever-increasing intensity, this obsessive, terrible desire to win at all costs—that so-called killer instinct that separates the champion from the dilettante. I think it all came to a head one day when I accidentally walked in on her in the training room and she had a life-size portrait of a man's head taped to the punching bag and was staring it in the eyes, screaming out "kill, kill, kill," and then pounding and pounding it into shreds with her bare fists. I tried calling the counsellor for advice, but we'd stopped paying him months ago and he wouldn't respond to any of my questions—bitter, I guess, because his idea had worked so well. There was just this long silence on the other end, until I said, "Okay, well I guess you haven't got any help for me." "Yes, thank you, goodbye," he replied.

I never spoke to her about that scene in the fitness room, and I don't think Smolinka saw me spying on her, but even *she* remarked, once or twice, on how she had this incredible blood-lust whenever we got into the ring, and how afterwards she just felt so good and relaxed and peaceful. "What worries me," Smolinka said one night, as we were lying in bed (the boxing had done wonders for our sex), "is that one day I'm going to kill you in a match and then I won't have anyone to celebrate with after-wards." She laughed, but I think I sensed a recognition there—that the two halves of her were becoming more and more irreconcilable, as if the boxing were driving her in conflicting directions, making her more nurturing at home and more homi-cidal in the ring, and that I was the emblem of this unappeasable contradiction. And I have to say that it did weird me out, the idea that my home life was so improved only because I had the shit beat out of me every week.

As with most obsessively pursued hobbies, Smolinka and I would talk non-stop about boxing at parties and dinners and afternoon coffees. At first, everyone was shocked, especially when we'd show up with cuts over our eyes, or tape across the bridges of our noses, wincing when we sat down, or not being able to turn properly to slam the car door—the visible effects of injury and overexertion—but eventually they began to notice that we weren't arguing any-more, that the "scenes" Smolinka and I had once staged at friends' places—such as yelling at each other, throwing dishes, asking the hosts and guests to take sides on an issue—were things of the past. And as old friends heard the rumours and reacquainted them-selves with us and began inviting us back to all those parties we'd been barred from, they began to ask how we'd done it—mainly because most of them were experiencing marital problems as well. So we'd tell them about the boxing.

I don't know how it happened, but soon enough we were host-ing boxing parties for married couples, and shortly thereafter Smolinka began working almost full eight-hour days to keep our fitness room up and running while husbands and wives came from all around to spar and train. We started making money at it; we started hosting tournaments; we found ourselves barely in control of a quickly growing business.

And for two years it grew, like craziness. Smolinka ran most of the training sessions, the workouts, the marathon "conditioning" workshops, and I tried my best to keep the books in order, to make sure that everyone got a receipt and that our accountant was kept up to speed on the climbing enrolment figures.

We had fun, too. There were weekly bouts, not only between Smolinka and myself but also other married couples, and afterwards there were beers and dinners and new friends. Smolinka and I were never better than in those twenty-four months, hammering each other in the ring and then, when that was over, passing the peroxide and band-aids back and forth between us, giving each other rubdowns, going for long jogs in the park every Saturday morning, and having sex at least once a day—all of which made our free fall out of boxing heaven that much more devastating. It's easy to go from bad to worse, but to go from bad to bliss and then back again, that's the worst.

Naturally, it was the religious groups. It started with a notice written up in the bulletin handed out every week at the Baptist Church, something about "blood sport," and "making a mockery of the sanctity of marriage," or some fundamentalist shit like that. That was fine. Nobody cared what Baptists thought, and, anyhow, they sucked in the ring. Pretty soon the Jehovahs got involved, which was even less of a blip on the radar screen. But once the news of our "violence therapy" reached the moral majority, and the local Roman Catholic and Anglican and United Church ministers jumped on the bandwagon, then we knew we were in for a flood. I think the end came when a supposedly former member of our gym sent an anonymous letter to the paper alleging that we had "encouraged violent confrontation over mediation," and that our philosophy of "brute force as a temporary solution to issues that really require a more 'spiritual' prescription went against all the dictates and messages underlying the Christian institution of marriage." The fact that we'd never suffered one single defection from our gym pretty much killed this "former member's" credibility; but my letters pointing this out, as well as elaborating our philosophy (that a "short-term solution" was often the best any marriage could hope for), must have gone straight into the editor's garbage can, proving Smolinka's contention that "the status quo has bricks in its gloves, and up its ass, too."

And, I have to hand it to her, Smolinka was the only one who stood up for us the day the cops showed up to check our "business licence." It turns out we were missing some trumped-up insurance papers, which our lawyers later informed us were completely unnecessary, but by then the raid had scared away all our customers and friends. I could see them filing out the door, heads bowed, shoulders slumped, not like fighters at all, with their stuffed duffle bags, their gloves roped together and dangling around their necks—hung up for good—while Smolinka raged at the police, dared them to get into the ring, threatened them with her fists, and finally refused to move from in front of our filing cabinets until four cops managed to grapple her to the floor and drag her out by the heels.

That was when I jumped in. I was worried, you see, because by then she was pregnant. That's right, somewhere along the line, between the sweating and punching and running and general happiness, Smolinka and I, or so she keeps assuring me, managed to get that egg fertilized. As a result, we took it easy the first three months—when things are precarious as far as fetal development is concerned—tapering down from full-contact matches to light sparring, wearing headgear, lightening up on the weights and cardio while upping the carbs and vegetables in our diet. But that night, once the cops had left and we were alone in the empty basement, surrounded by scattered files, the chaotic mess of weights and machines, the smell of concrete mould and the lingering echo of grunts and body blows, Smolinka turned to me and nodded toward the ring.

It was not our usual fight, full of the preening and cursing, the ringside cheers and laughter of friends—my quiet determination, Smolinka's showmanship. This one was grim. And it took place in grainy darkness, without the lights that were usually glaring down from overhead, as if there was nothing between us at all—no friendship, no marriage, no business—nothing but the bond that brings opponents together. Or so it seemed at first, as I bounced up and down on my toes, moving against Smolinka, who became uncharacteristically silent after the bell went off.

We went one round, two, three, four. By the sixth we were covered in sweat, and I was starting to get worried for the baby, aiming my shots high, at her nose and chest. I tried raising my eyebrows at her a few times but she just shook her head and continued zeroing in, wide-shouldered, like a walking block of cement. We continued through rounds seven, eight, nine, ten, up against the limits of exhaustion, both of us staggering around the ring, skimming hits off shoulders and foreheads, coming together in clinches that lasted longer and longer. I was drinking masses of water between rounds just to keep my mouth unstuck, and it was slowing me down, forcing me to concentrate more than ever on predicting where her next blow would come from, and where she wanted it to land. Smolinka, meanwhile, had turned into a tank, dispensing with finesse and strategy to rely on her size and intensity to wear me down, wiring her shots along direct, economical lines—like the signatures of a man in a blindfold.

It wasn't until the twelfth round that I decided I didn't want the fight to end, that I was happy to keep dancing like this until my lungs gave way, or my heart, or my bones, because it seemed—in complete contradiction of how I'd felt at the start of the bout—that by fighting each other Smolinka and I were actually *fighting together*—against despair, foreclosure, impossibility—as if the blows we landed were accumulating somewhere else, raining down on some distant, invisible enemy whose body was hers and mine combined.

But Smolinka, as usual, was on another wavelength. In the fifteenth round, as we clinched for maybe the thirtieth time, she said something she'd never said before, despite all the accusations aimed at me over the years. She whispered in my ear, "It's not your baby." She might as well have pulled a Tyson and ripped my ear off with her teeth, because I was so stunned (though my subconscious must have suspected this all along) that I stepped back, letting down my guard for the second it took her to drop me with a hard jab to the teeth.

That was my second concussion.

I woke to tears—not just my own. Smolinka was kneeling above me, her gloved hands cradling the back of my head, sobbing as she said over and over, "It's a lie, it's a lie, it's a lie."

I never came back over to believing it was my kid. Smolinka tried everything to win me over, even going to a doctor for DNA testing. But I was skeptical because the sheet she brought home seemed to have been altered, in that careful, exacting hand I'd seen her use on report cards back in high school.

Yes, we've been together since high school. I know that would seem impossible to anyone watching us now—two high school sweethearts, one of them eight months pregnant, duking it out with prize-fighting ferocity—but that's how it was when we got together: the girl who was taller and stronger than most of the neighbourhood boys and the guy who was maybe the most unobtrusive person in the history of grade twelve. She wasn't so much popular as dreaded, especially by the other girls, but nobody realized that her anger and violence were a result of what she'd always encountered—the kid with the funny Russian name, the funny Russian parents, who didn't know what to do when the other kids always backed away until she had no choice but to give them exactly what they feared. My willingness to get into the ring, to go all the way without backing out, has kept us together for years.

Even now, in round eight, I'm thinking of how she was back then as I circle away from her jabs and try to avoid being KO'd for the twenty-first time. I'm moving in and moving out. Getting nowhere.

And then it occurs to me that hitting her in the stomach might kill all kinds of birds, get rid of the baby and possibly give me a much-needed knockout. I'm not sure where this thought comes from, and am not even sure it comes from me (though where else would it have come from?) but there it is: rising out of my subconscious like a twisted little directive, when I thought I'd long ago put Smolinka's betrayal behind me, when I'd already decided I didn't care whether she was lying about my paternity.

And I step toward her, not sure whether I've decided to do it, but just to see if she's left that kind of opening in her defence—to see whether it would be *possible* for me to KO the baby. But I make two mistakes: having succeeded in threading her defence I hesitate at the critical moment, drawing back from the blow I should have landed, and, in my hesitation, leaving myself open to Smolinka, who, intensely maternal and willing to credit everyone else with her own underhandedness, steps quickly to the side and brings her killer left up onto the point of my chin.

And from there on in it's stars. I'm aware of being down, of struggling to get onto all fours while Smolinka stands looking down at me (why isn't she bouncing around—I wonder dimly— readying herself to deliver that final, crushing blow?). And I'm gazing into the glimmering distance, into the spaces between each pinprick of light swirling round my cranium, thinking how terrible it is that most of the universe is just darkness, all that room and only a star here or there to break the monotony. But the realization is too easy, and I rise away from it, angling my body as I get up to avoid a possible roundhouse (Smolinka's favourite blow).

And she's just standing there, back straight, arms limp, her eyes following mine as I bounce around, my fists up, wondering what new, hellish tactic of hers this is.

"Go ahead," she says, rubbing her fists ineffectually against her thighs.

"What?"

"Just do it!"

My bouncing decreases until I, too, come to a stop, all energy gone, as the dark light of the ring washes over us, and I sense, suddenly, that this *is* the final attack in a fight whose relevance far exceeds the ring, that will be fought only once, and allow neither encore nor rematch. It is a fight Smolinka intends to win.

She murmurs, "If it's not your baby, then you might as well."

I pull my fist back, staring at her, who's staring at me, sweat now pouring off her face, almost trickling into the front of her shirt—as if her whole body were convulsing, every pore squeezing out its tears—while I pull my right fist back and take a small step toward her, my left fist raised as a shield in case she tries anything. Smolinka winces, expecting a blow, but her guard remains down.

We stand like that for a full minute, neither of us wavering, and then I strike out with both fists, hitting her on either shoulder, forcing her to resume the boxing stance. And I'm so relieved to see the sudden smile in her eyes, and to know that the baby is mine and that I wasn't capable of hurting it either way, that I can't help but feel a surge of confidence, which translates into a nervous energy as we bounce around the ring, both of us grinning through our mouthpieces and looking for the openings that will let us score just a few more points.

Radio Blik

I'D LIKE TO BELIEVE THAT before he died Leon Blik perfected the
art of writing in ruins. The truth, however, is that he had no choice
but to write as he did, each sentence demanded of him by the
knowledge of his approaching death, at 57, from cancer. And,
probably, my need to see his final journal as an *intentional* work—
a product of wilful effort—is because I can't bear the thought of
what it must have been like, watching meaning disintegrate even as
he scrawled it upon the page.

You see, I stole Blik's final journal, along with one of the radios,
from his cellar workshop, and drove from his house to Holman's
Ridge, where I lay down in the back seat of my car and read it. It
seems ridiculous to me now, hiding out like that, but at the time I
was worried that Helena, having discovered what I'd done, might
be angry enough to follow me up there and tear the journal from
my hands, returning it to the man Blik had intended it for. As it
was, Helena did find out I'd stolen it, though only much later, after
I'd spent weeks and weeks poring over my friend's last sentences,
and holding the plug of the last radio he'd "repaired," scared that if
I put it into the socket I'd electrocute myself. And, anyway, Helena
wasn't even angry.

It is not easy, reading the journal of a dead friend, and even harder
when it's written in sentences that don't ever come to an end,
clause upon clause upon clause, until you lose all sense of what the
writer is trying to say, until the writer himself seems so exasperated
at his failure to communicate that he can't, in good faith, put a

period to anything. Having lost the way, or his point, Blik would turn the page when the sentence he'd been trying to complete ground to a halt, and begin an entirely new version. As a result, the journal read like someone trying to revise the same sentence over and over. But it was exactly this that kept me in suspense: would Blik, on the very final page, at last complete his thought?

Well, I never did close the book. I left it there in frustration, in the back seat of my car, open to that last sheet of lined paper, the words staring at the ceiling as if waiting for a drop of ink, aimed just right, to splash down and supply the missing period. And while I've gone back through that journal many times, checking out the words, copying out the phrases, even reading them aloud into the still air, when I'm done I always leave the spiral-ring binder as it was: open, its words exposed, lingering on the horizon of one last idea.

I suppose if I had to put the experience into words, I would say that reading Blik's last journal is like standing in a vast field of stones and suddenly noticing that carved into each is a fragment of pattern—a rose, a fish, a cross—only to realize there are too many fragments, too many possible combinations, to ever connect them. And this is what makes me hang onto the journal, this feeling that the words have less to do with Blik's father, or even about the kinds of expression trauma wrings from us, than with the fact that, in the effort to purify the writing, to arrive at a message from which all traces of the author—his longing, his inadequacy, his *sentiment*— had been stripped away, Blik accomplished the opposite. So that what reading produces is less a sense of Blik's negation than the impossible distance between the two of you, which only makes you feel that he's out there somewhere, vitally present, and your job is to somehow get back to him.

It is a book about distance, and, as such, it belongs to anyone.

...

Apart from his writing, Blik's other fascination was radio, though these two things were not mutually exclusive, as he explained that day in his basement when I first visited him. There were wide workbenches along every wall, and on these a tangle of wires and speakers and antennas and crystals, so much of it piled up, and so high, it was a wonder Blik could find a single thing he was looking for; or clear himself a space in which to work; or even move out of the room when he was finished for the day, when he'd successfully reassembled his radios, which sat in such numbers on the floor: tiny portables with wrist straps, kitchen-counter varieties, antique radios as tall as the average man.

In fact, what Blik did that first day was sidle and climb, moving nimbly for a man of his age, until he reached the one vacant spot in the midst of all that clutter, where there was just room enough for his two feet to stand underneath a square foot of empty work-bench. Along the way he'd turned on all the radios that worked, so that by the time he reached his destination it seemed as if Blik no more wanted to leave room for his body in the midst of all those spare parts than for his voice amidst the competing babble of static and music and announcements. He was yelling something above the roar of frequencies, opening his mouth and repeating the same phrase over and over. I cupped a hand to my ear and shook my head to indicate I couldn't hear a word.

Whereupon Blik reached up and hit a switch on the wall beside him, cutting all power to the room, leaving the two of us in a silence so sudden and dark the room was thick with it, and I had the sensation of not being able to move, or call out, of barely being able to breathe. It was as if the air around us had turned to amber.

"When I was a child," said Blik, in his soft, unwavering mono-tone, "my father showed me how to build a crystal radio." He paused. My eyes began to make out some of the shapes in the room. "He went away, you know," continued Blik, "and I remem-ber sitting there—oh, I must have been six or seven—tuning and tuning that radio, convinced that if I hit the right frequency I might find his voice revealing where he'd gone, or the directions to finding him. Maybe the time of his return. Though after a while all I expected were the reasons for why he'd left."

As a child he was often amazed, Blik admitted, to find there were so many sources—almost infinite—transmitting information across the airwaves. In all that space there must have existed the possibility of tuning in to his father's voice. Blik said he spent hours with that radio, lengthening the wire coil around the bleach bottle, creating more taps to tune into greater numbers of stations, adding to the length of his antenna every time he came upon suitable wire. "Oh, I know why he left," said Blik. "I think I knew even then. It had to do with nerves. I remember coming upon him at times, angrily speaking to himself. A lot of people—a very few, I mean—they get trapped. They run out of help. But I did not want to think it was the effect my mother and us kids had upon him."

It was still dark in Blik's workshop, though I could now make out his shape against a wall of indiscernible tools, his hand on the switch, ready to turn the power on again, to drown his voice in a wail of radios, should anything he say betray him.

He paused, and then abruptly changed the subject. "Walter Benjamin. You've read 'Art in the Age of Mechanical Reproduction'? He spoke of film. The thesis suggests it lends itself to certain . . . fascist effects. And, of course, much has been said about the way that Hitler and Mussolini used the radio to similar ends . . ." He trailed off, then laughed as he remembered something. "As a child I used to speak into the radio, imagining . . . as if my father was out there, listening, and he could hear me." Blik cleared his throat. "But of course radios only transmit one way. They don't care an iota for what you have to say. Information is theirs. And even when it isn't . . . even their silence is an instruction, a *command*. Even then you are being told something that requires you not to respond, merely receive, without acknowledgment or question." And with this, Blik grimaced. I could see the light from outside glancing off his teeth. Then he flipped the switch again, and for several minutes I was blinded by the lights, deafened by the roar.

Holman's Ridge is a two-hour drive from town—level ground of some four square miles a hundred feet above sea level, from the edges of which they launch hang-gliders and weather balloons. The drop is sheer. It is the place I drove to that Thanksgiving— rolling hills flecked red and gold, white clouds sharply defined, the daylit moon less a milestone than a reminder of what the infinite does to all measures. Standing on the edge, I turned around to get my fill of those distances, as if they might console me, or provide an antidote to that terrible claustrophobia we'd felt sitting by Blik's bed in the intensive care ward, every rustle of the tubes and wires attached to his body affecting us like the thrashing of a torture vic- tim beyond our help, until his sister, Helena, leaned over and told Blik that his friends were all here, and that he'd fought for so long, and that he could go. Blik closed his eyes. "Thank you, thank you," he whispered. The last words before he left.

As I said, it was at Holman's Ridge that I first leafed through the final journal. I'd put it into my shirt minutes before the arrival of Blik's two nephews, who'd been sent to gather up Blik's writings and deliver them to the "distant relative"—Blik's father—who'd shown up out of the blue at the funeral, and who was as surprised as we were angered by the fact that Blik had bequeathed to him every last word he'd written. It had been a weird, sentimental gesture on Blik's part, and had struck me, Helena, and all of Blik's closest friends and relatives like an act of violence—as if a gift had been torn from us and given to a man wholly undeserving. I watched as the nephews kicked aside the radios littering the floor to get to the shelves and desk, which were wedged into a corner of the basement, where they roughly lifted the books and dumped them into several cardboard cartons, emptied the filing cabinet, reached up for the row of identical notebooks, their spines bound in red leather, that occupied an entire shelf above Blik's desk, and from which I'd stolen the final volume just a moment before. I stood there, watching them, wishing I'd had more time to stuff my shirt full of books.

But the truth is, the final journal was the only work of Blik's I wanted, having listened to Helena over the phone for too many nights during the final stages of his illness, listening to her complain about how "Leon [was] running himself down, just sitting in his room in front of that journal all night, writing the same line over and over." There were scenes, I knew, during the final weeks of Blik's illness, times when he'd lock himself in the workshop to concentrate unmolested on his sentence, Helena pounding at the door, "near hysterical," as she admitted to me at Blik's funeral, "knowing how little time we had left, and how Leon refused to share it."

Later, however, some months after Blik was laid to rest, as we sat together one night in her kitchen drinking wine, Helena admitted, "It was just death, really. Just that I couldn't see any way out of it, couldn't see what Leon needed in order to cope. It's funny, you know," she said, staring into her wineglass, "but most people would want to be around family at a time like that. My brother just wanted to be alone . . . with his sentence . . . his radios. And I guess I was selfish enough to be afraid, even though it was *his* death." She paused, swirling her wine around. "Or is that wrong? I wonder sometimes, you know, whether our deaths, of all things, should be ours to do with as we like, or whether they're the one thing we *must* share with those around us." I sat for some time across from her, the surface of the table dark in the absence of an overhead lamp, and heavy to the point of breaking with the question she'd placed upon it. I had no answer for her then, though it's just as possible she didn't want one, having sent it out—uttered it into dead air— knowing there was no suitable response.

...

After the nephews left with Blik's books, the men from the radio shop arrived, though not before I'd had a chance to poke around the workshop a little more, flipping switches, turning dials, bending antennas back and forth for better reception, putting my ear to speakers as if Blik had left me the task of listening. After the men finally arrived, were led downstairs by Helena, introduced to me as "a friend helping to clear Leon's junk," and shown around the room, they began to look at the radios and smile, holding back from open laughter at first, probably out of respect for the dead, though finally unable to restrain themselves.

"Hey, Theo, check this out," one of the men whispered, chuckling. The echo of the basement, now emptied of Blik's books and manuscripts, magnified every laugh. "Take a look at this." He pointed to a radio Blik must have been working on shortly before his death, occupying the space where he normally worked. "What do you think that is?" the man asked.

Theo bent over and gazed at the back of the radio, where the back panel had been removed. He turned it into the light and poked at the wires with a screwdriver taken from a peg on the wall. "It's like he was trying to turn the receiver inside out," he said, shaking his head in amazement. "Everything's the wrong way around." He gave the radio's innards another poke or two, and then straightened up.

After their inspection I could hear them talking to Helena upstairs, telling her some of the units could be refurbished, once they'd "undone" the damage caused by Blik's "repairs," but that most were little good for anything but spare parts. Helena said she just wanted everything gone and would be happy to take whatever they offered, provided the basement was emptied by the end of the week. While they were speaking I went over to the bench and lifted Blik's last radio, bundling it into a garbage bag. I then opened one of the dirty windows of the cellar, set high in the walls and level with the ground outside, and pushed the package through, setting it down gently in the grass. Upon leaving, I went around and retrieved it.

Plugging it in later that evening, I blew every fuse in the house. The spark thrown off by the wall socket was so large my wife and youngest daughter (the only one of our seven children still living at home) actually saw it from where they were watching TV in the next room, and came running into my study to make sure I was all right. I was, of course, though only physically. Because down in *my* basement, while fumbling with a flashlight and the fuses, I held my hand on the switch, unable, or perhaps unwilling, to bring the lights back on. What had Blik been doing? Despite the mockery of the repairmen—a ruse to make Helena and me think Blik's junk was worthless—I knew Blik had at least a basic competence when it came to radios, which meant the last one he'd worked on was not misrepaired but sabotaged. But who was the intended target of this? And for what reason? Blik had spent the last days of his life turning a radio inside out, as if it were some kind of animal whose throat you could reach into, grabbing the guts and pulling them upwards, bending the jaws back until it was shiny purple and pink on the outside and fur-lined within. I couldn't imagine the sort of anguish—physical, mental—that could have made him turn against the work he loved. And because I couldn't imagine it, I felt there had to be some answer other than the obvious: that Blik's mind had been so clouded by the emotional turmoil of dying that he'd started gutting radios, and leaving his precious writing to the wrong man. No, I preferred fixating on his last, inexplicable acts in the form of a question.

Not that the answer was forthcoming. In fact, it seemed to recede from me day and night. The more time I spent in my study staring at the radio, or studying manuals on radio repair, or reading the unending sentences in Blik's journal, the more I felt the answer wouldn't be achieved by concentrating on these relics left behind, and the more I felt like jumping in the car and driving up to Holman's Ridge—until it was only with my eyes fixed on those impossible panoramas, their unaccountable distances, that I felt released from the information Blik had left (that he *continued* to leave), and the way it made me feel.

Of course, the journal was right there with me, and the moment I relaxed I had to open it up, destroying all that peace those distances brought.

It was only a matter of time before Helena found out what I'd done. I was in my office on the northwest corner of the top floor of the McLaren Building, at three o'clock on a Friday afternoon, when she walked in.

Now, not everyone can simply walk into my office. You have to climb through a bank of secretaries just to get to the front door, which is usually closed. You have to answer at least two questions, "What's your name?" and "Do you have an appointment?" to which an answer of nothing to the first, or a "No" to the second, guarantees my privacy. If you're intent on getting through without either of these passwords, then it's best to start with surveillance, making sure I'm in the office, followed by a fast attack: rushing to the doorknob and bursting into the room with the secretaries hot on your heels.

Which is exactly what Helena did. "Owen, you stole it!"

"You're not allowed in there," shrieked Marilyn, coming into my office a second after Helena, and grabbing her arm.

"It's okay, Marilyn." I rose quietly from behind the sales forecasts I'd been looking at and gestured weakly toward the door. Marilyn looked at me a second, then at Helena, and then turned back with a questioning look. I nodded and she very carefully turned and shut the door as she left. The click of the latch seemed to last several seconds longer than it normally did.

"Why?" said Helena, not moving from the spot where she'd stopped.

I lifted up the sales forecast sheets and picked up the open journal underneath. "I can't . . ." I held the journal in my open hands
for a while, unable to speak, and then closed and pushed it across
the desk. She made no move toward it.

I sighed, still standing by the desk, and lifted, for a few seconds,
my hands to either cheek. "You know how many brothers and sisters I had, Helena?" She looked at me, but I could see she was beginning to let her shoulders drop to normal level. "Eleven." I laughed.
"One of my earliest memories is wandering around the house with
a book in my hand, looking for a place to read, stepping into all
these rooms to find them filled. Hostile glances. Everyone thinking
I was planning to violate the kingdoms they'd established, meas-
ured out in square feet. Everyone pretending the others weren't
there. And then here I come, wanting to make even *less* room.

"We weren't poor or anything, at least relatively. There were just
a lot of us. What do you call the opposite of loneliness?" I asked
Helena, looking across at the book and shaking my head. "What is
that? I've been trying to think. . . ." I bit my lip. "Since Blik died I've
been trying to think of it. . . ."

And in a second, as fast as she'd burst into my office, Helena was
there by the desk, wrapping me in an embrace, her arms encircling
my own, which dangled uselessly by my sides. But it took me only
a second to break free and move to the opposite half of the desk.
"No," I shook my head. "I don't want that right now," I said,
unnerved by the feeling that the consolation she offered wasn't
meant for me but, in some way, for Blik, for the part of her brother
she was seeing in me.

"I need to finish," I said. "When Father Infante married June and
me, I remember wishing my mother and father could have been
there; I remember missing all that family, scattered or dead or
feuding. Seven years, seven kids later, I'm waking mornings in the
back seat of the car, wandering into the house to find June on the
couch with Billy. Mary and Louise are in our room. Everyone in
the wrong bed. I think we'd all gotten about three hours sleep,

especially June and me, wandering from one crying kid's bedroom to the next, trying to keep them from waking each other.

"And then it's in to work, sitting out there," I gestured at the wall, meaning the large room beyond, where the copy pool toiled over their word processors and allotted fragments of advertising. "Sitting out there . . . it was like some dream factory, Helena. That's what that job did to you. You started turning the work into something else." I laughed. "You know I studied literature at university? It's why they hired me. They wanted someone who could pump out clean sentences. And that's what I did, day after day, polishing them and polishing them and polishing them, as if I could turn copy into literature. It's what trauma does, you know. And it *is* trauma, or a form of it: doing that work for years, trying to ignore the time. You find little rituals, ways of controlling your corner of the world. Token acts that help you shut out what's controlling *you*.

"There was a guy there. Joe Racky. I still don't know if that was his real name. A mathematician. I can see him staring at sheets of paper, trying to come up with a formula that would allow him to figure out how much copy he'd churned out in a day. Louise Morillo. She was into breaking her own record. Working at a million miles an hour, trying to outdo however much she'd managed to do the day before. Oh, she didn't care about the work. Just the challenge. It was how she managed to get through the day.

"Blik was my boss back then. But he had ten years on me. I'm sorry," I said, stopping. "I'm going too fast; it's all jumbled." I walked over to one of the cupboards in my office and took out a bottle hidden behind a bunch of empty folders, two paper cups stolen from the stack beside the water dispenser. I poured drinks. Helena unfolded her arms and took up the cup but didn't lift it to her lips. In the end, I didn't drink from mine either, walking over to the window and turning my back to her.

"I was obsessive." I laughed. "Still am, actually. But back then I thought I could . . . get out of my situation, that if I was patient enough my kids would learn to look after themselves, that I would discover a few lost hours to the day—over and above the twenty-four—when I could fill out some applications for graduate school, work on my writing, even just sit and read ten pages in a row. I honestly thought it would work out, that this soul-crushing situation was just temporary. But you know how the years go. . . . After a while you're not even thinking that way anymore. You've forgotten how much you wanted. Or, rather, your consciousness has forgotten, though the rest of the brain goes on dreaming.

"In my third year or so I started writing these sentences. They were long things. . . ." I laughed. "I think I'd read an article on Proust. I used to read *The New York Times Book Review* whenever my kids let me sit on the toilet for more than ten seconds at a time. I remember it, though I don't think that what happened to me, in the end, had much to do with Proust. It could have been anything. The article talked about how Proust didn't write sequentially— like most of us do—from beginning to end. Instead, he wrote in three dimensions: clause interrupting clause interrupting clause, until you felt like you were falling through a series of trapdoors, as if you were travelling not across the page but *into* it. And I started writing these sentences at work. I don't know why," I said. "It was what a lot of other people were doing: finding a way to personalize the job. I just started playing around with how long and complicated I could make the copy."

"When the deadline came I'd have to hand it to Racky. He was like the rest of us: someone who's got a real knack for suffering in silence; the kind of person who can't articulate his rage. He'd just take it from me and whittle away the sentences. The sentences, in the meantime, got longer, and he'd be looking at me out of the corner of his eye as we worked. I don't know . . . I think at first I thought I could do both: do a bit of writing at work and still churn out what the company wanted. But the more I worked on the writing the more fixated I got, until it crowded out everything else." I laughed again. "I don't know what I was thinking, really. I don't recall consciously trying to turn all that dreck into literature. But that's what I was attempting, in effect." I turned toward Helena, and saw a film of scotch on her upper lip.

"Of course it fell apart. I don't know what it was. Maybe the looks from Racky, which by then were pretty much straight on, as if he'd discovered he did have a capacity for anger after all.

"One day I just put my head down on the page. I couldn't finish the sentence. Tried it a hundred ways. The more I fiddled the longer it grew. The longer it grew the more options there were. I was exhausted."

Helena put her empty cup down on my desk. "That's how you became friends with Blik."

"He didn't need to be sitting out there with us in the pool. He could have had his own office." I pointed at the wall again. "The present manager has his own office. But Blik wanted to be with us. And not because he liked to keep his eye on things. I think he worked better when there were other people around. Company. Not that we ever treated him like one of us. Alone but apart: that's how Blik liked it. Anyhow, he saw my head on the desk and took me outside."

"Blik never told me why he'd taken an interest, and it took me quite a while to understand it. He just invited us over. All of us— June, the kids, me. It seems like we were there every weekend, or every other weekend, at least. After a while he put up swings in his backyard. A sandbox. As the kids got older he'd take them sledding, swimming. As for us: he gave June and me that room at the top of the third floor—what would eventually become your bedroom. Said we could sleep, or write, or whatever. I remember the first time: June and I just sat in there together, on the bed. We'd get up to check on the kids and Blik would wave us away. We'd go back to the room. It took a while to get used to it. Eventually June stopped coming; she found other things to do, elsewhere. That's when I brought in the books and the desk, though I never got much done. Mainly, I slept. It helped me get myself together at work. Promotions." I gestured around my office. "That kind of thing." I had walked from the window to the back of my chair by this point, grabbing the backrest and swivelling it lightly from side to side, as if I was proud of the chair, wanting to show it off to best effect. "I never really understood why Blik did it until you moved in," I said. "God, I didn't even understand when he first showed me the radios!"

"Leon was lonely," said Helena. "He was always lonely."

"Even before . . . well, before. . . ."

"Before our father left?" Helena looked at the journal on the desk. "Whenever I think of Leon, now, or back then. . . . Even in my earliest memories Leon is lonely. He loved being around your kids. I think him asking me to move in, following my divorce . . . well, it had more to do with missing them."

But I wasn't listening to the last part of Helena's speech, thinking instead of that terrible verb tense, "Leon *is* lonely," as if even now, on the other side of life, Blik was still sitting in some dank cellar, twisting a tuning knob, desperate for an incoming message. And then it occurred to me, remembering him around my kids, how Blik's face wore his expectation back then, looking at them as if his ear were bent to one of those radios, as if what he wanted was neither loneliness nor company, but an affection whose measure was the distance between people. It was as if, for him, loneliness had come to mean presence. Maybe it's what he'd come to love, having been denied his father: the consolation of space, a separation so vast you'd need a million antennas to make contact, each word spoken into the speaker as poignant and ludicrous as prayers for the dead. I once joked with him that he should invest in ham radio, in a medium where you could actually make transmissions, and he gazed at me with an expression that is only now beginning to make sense: the look of a boy who's been denied contact so long he has come to love the only thing that connects him to his father: the authority of voices that speak without listening, that communicate without engaging in dialogue. The dead air of a distance across which nothing can travel. I suppose this is why Blik looked relieved when the children and I left: not because he wanted us gone, but because he'd spent too long with anticipation not to prefer it. It was a distortion of character—his consolation—a place you come to after considerable harm. And I'd failed to see it.

"Blik never told me why your father left," I said to Helena.

"Because we didn't know why," she replied, "though Blik always felt we'd had an explanation, once, but that he was too young at the time to understand it, and since then everyone else had forgotten."

"That's crazy."

"Yes," she said, smiling indulgently. "But, you know, he didn't talk about it much. My brother was a sweetheart. Eccentric, but a sweetheart." She looked down at the journal. "What are you planning on doing with that?"

I started to say something, to tell Helena I planned to return it to her father, but something stopped me, and instead I said, "The way it's written. Those sentences. Have you read them?"

She shook her head. "They were meant for someone else."

Had I known this? Had I realized the extent of my theft? "The radio too?"

"I think so," she answered. "Although I didn't realize it until I spoke to June, and she told me you'd shut the whole house down plugging it in. It was an emblem of some kind. For all I know, the journal and the radio were meant to go together," Helena said. "But if you or the radio repairmen hadn't taken it, I would have thrown it in the garbage."

"So Blik never told you?"

"I think he meant to," she answered. "He said there were still some 'important things' he wanted to say. But it all happened too fast." Helena looked at the empty whisky cup in her hand, and I moved quickly to fill it. "When I first gave my father the journals he just looked at them. And when he noticed the last one was missing he started to cry." Helena shrugged. "It seemed appropriate to me, at first, those tears, as if that's what Blik had meant to do to him.

My father and I didn't talk much, Owen. Maybe his trail never went cold for Leon, but it went cold for me a long time ago."

"Do you want me to send it to him?"

"I don't know," she shrugged again. "I didn't get his address. Is there anything interesting there?"

"It's some kind of announcement, something Blik's trying to broadcast," I said. "But he spends the whole journal rewriting it without ever quite managing to finish. Anyhow," I gestured at myself, "it reminds me, that way, in its being unfinished, of that breakdown I had. It reminds me of Blik's help."

"You'd better keep it, then," said Helena. "And the radio."

I drove up to Holman's Ridge that afternoon following work, thinking, as my car threaded the switchbacks, of a recent book I'd read that had argued for "sentimentality" being the greatest crime of the twentieth century. Apparently, or so the author said, Hitler and his followers had been great sentimentalists. It wasn't a new argument, by any stretch, though calling sentimentality a "crime" and equating it with Nazism showed a kind of superficial originality. And, yet, once again at the top of the ridge, gazing into that empty space and watching teenagers bank their kites—which were flying way out at the end of strings and down along the rock walls—I couldn't help but wonder: what else is there, really, other than sentiment? *Especially at the end.* What good were those logics of vertical steel, facts harder and clearer than diamonds, visions so sober-eyed they went beyond all considerations of the heart, when, in the last second of the last morning of the last day, all you really wanted was a voice saying you'd done what you could, and that it was okay to go? When all you wanted was to feel as if someone was watching, no matter how far away? It must have seemed to Blik, as it seemed to me then, that sentimentality was the clearest realization of all: an acknowledgment of the loss and desire we spend our lives denying, mainly through these pastimes—reason, logic, objectivity—that give us no more hold on our lives, in the end, than their opposites. For what is logic, finally, but a mind longing to bridge the distance?

And I did not know the answer to Helena's question, whether our death is something we *should* share with others; I knew only that we are not able, in the end, to keep it to ourselves.

Yes, I kept the journal. The radio. And sentiment is my only justification. Because even now you might find me—nights when my wife and daughter are away, when the house is my own, when I don't have to worry about flipping back the fuse—sitting in front of Blik's plugged-in radio and reading his journal into that inverted speaker, as if death were a message I could reply to, as if Blik's idea of heaven was to be waiting there, on the other side, his ear still pressed to the speaker.

The Inert Landscapes
of György Ferenc

For Bill New

MY FATHER WAS a landscape painter in a nation that would not be reproduced. When he looked out over the forests and oceans, the lakes and rivers, even the clouds and mists, all he saw was a blank slate, a landscape so deprived of the associations and history he was used to that his brush was always poised above the canvas, stalled in the act. His tragedy, I suppose, was that for him Canada had become a place of exile, a removal from the one country—Hungary—that had always spoken to him, so insistent with its colours and forms it was as if the geography, not he, were dictating the speed of the brushstrokes.

The archetypal moment, the one that encapsulates my father's relations with Canada, is that rainy September day in 1954 when he walked over for an afternoon tea and paused in the entryway to my apartment, staring at a print I had received from one of my students. I was teaching art history by then, at the Toronto College of Design (where I still work)—having been hired for my "anti-totalitarian perspective"—and spending a lot of time at the local bar with the men and women enrolled in my Survey of Western Art course, many of whom were also in the visual arts program, or working artists.

I was sharing the apartment with the woman who was to become my wife, Marguerite, a former student who went on to become a schoolteacher, and that September day we were both standing behind my father as he appraised the print. It showed a water tower erected in a town up the coast that was not unfamiliar, because it was where our family had first settled after my father got us out of Hungary by flashing from the car a set of ration booklets the guards mistook for passports, waving us through in advance of less-resourceful refugees. (This was just months before the Iron Curtain clanged down, preventing Hungarians from going west, and transforming the job of border guard from document inspector to sniper .) The town in the print, Stillwater, was our first home after the Austrian camps, and though we lived there only a few years before moving to Vancouver, it was a time of peace for my family, filled with the exhilaration of having come through fire unsinged; of finding ourselves in a country where we could express our dislike of the government, read what books we liked, pursue studies along non-official lines; where my father could again produce his "bourgeois" landscapes, many of them so abstract they'd been banned as "decadent" or "ahistorical" by the Nazi and Soviet art censors.

The water tower was printed in deep blue and black, the pipes and metal siding of the container contrasting with the darkness the artist had ascribed to the surrounding brush and forest. My father looked at it from a few different angles, and then said, "It's not bad, but it would be better if he dropped the title." I hadn't noticed the name of the print before, and bent down to look at it, only to find, in pencil just underneath the author's signature, "Stillwater Tower, 1953, 5/25." When I asked my father why the title was problematic he couldn't really come up with a response, shrugging his shoulders and muttering something to the effect that it was a water tower meant to provide water, and that he remembered seeing a lot of rust on it, which reminded him of a nearby parking lot, and that there was a "profound lack of poetry in Stillwater"; in short, like the rest of Canada he'd encountered, there wasn't any spirit there, just a kind of banality he referred to as "square." "This country," he frequently said, "is art-resistant."

This was his dominant theme. No matter how good the wine was, no matter how smooth its taste, if it came from someplace such as South Africa or California it could only ever be second rate; and if it had a name like "Bill Bart's Estate," or "Otter Pine

Ridge Cabernet," or "Frank McMillan Chardonnay," then it would never, ever, ever be good wine—sorry. "How can you take seriously a wine that goes by the name of Bill Bart?" my father would ask. "No, no," and he'd shake his head. It was the same with everything. Glenn Gould's fame, for instance, my father was certain, derived entirely from the fact that he was Canadian, because Canada just didn't have many good artists and so had to elevate to cultural prominence the few mediocrities it produced (in Hungary, he insisted, players of Gould's calibre were "to be found on every street corner"); and, besides, his first name was Glenn, for God's sake! Who'd ever heard of anyone being able to play classical music well, never mind being worthy of playing it in the first place, whose name was Glenn? "No," my father said, "I'm sorry, but it's quite impossible." That's not to say there weren't moments, he admitted, when, listening to Gould, he'd almost be lulled into liking the music, almost forget where it was coming from, but then it would occur to him that the guy playing was called Glenn, and that would be it.

And it was the same with my print: the minute the image suggested anything Canadian, the magic or mystery or art would vanish and it became a living reminder of how lacking this country was, how it was not "founded," how it was without ethos, without lexicon—just a terrible mishmash of British "squarehead" thinking and Hollywood "pop culture"—and how far removed my father was from the place where real culture, real art even had the possibility of being produced: namely, Europe. "They just don't have it," he would sigh. "And it's not something you can cultivate." This was a country where you could work, where you could find the necessary isolation, but it was not a place that lent itself to art because to have art you needed a vocabulary that bespoke "spirit." Here, the mountains were only mountains, the rivers only rivers, the lakes only lakes. They spoke of nothing but themselves and so remained objects of blank utility, not "coexistent"—by which he meant that for landscape painting to be possible one must have the sense that the geography and the people of a country weren't *relative to one another* but *were one another*—that landscape and citizen, like ghosts, were mixing their atoms in order to occupy the same spot at the same time—and that this was especially evident in the names given to Canadian geography, which seemed to him inappropriate, tossed off, distilled from woefully ordinary activities such as logging, fishing, and hunting.

"Every nation logs and fishes and hunts," he'd say, "so what?" You could switch the names around and you'd still have the same mountain, same lake, same water tower. But take the "Szabadság" out of Szabadsághegy in Budapest and suddenly there would be a crater where Freedom Mount (he hated these sorts of translations, by the way) had once stood. Paradoxically, the same terms he deplored in English "sounded right somehow" in German, Italian or Hungarian, as if the sonorities of those languages were productive of the spirit, the sense of oneness, that names such as Mount Logan could never conjure up.

And my father had been very successful back there. The famous Hungarian critic, Bruno Keles, wrote, in his canonical treatise, *The Budapest Circle*, that "György Ferenc is the most perceptive of our landscape painters; in his work one sees the absence of a dividing line between a geography and its people, or, rather, one senses the inextricability of geography and the soul. His paintings are at once celebratory and melancholy because they recognize the fragility of a nation in its incapacity to survive the removal of its frontiers, the transformation of its names, the evaporation of its colours."

He and our entire family suffered horrible abuse under the fascists, particularly once the Arrow Cross Party came to power in 1944; and things were no better under the Communist regime, when our family was kicked out of our Budapest apartment (where we'd lived, during the last year of the war, under house arrest, as a result of my father's stature as a nationalist and the various inflammatory statements he'd made against the Nazis), and relocated to a small town south of Debrecen, to a tiny, poorly insulated home that we were sure had once served, more efficiently, as a henhouse. There, we lasted only four months before my father packed us into a Fiat aimed at Austria.

While my father had been incredibly popular in Hungary— even during the war years and days of house arrest—in Canada he was, by his own estimation, "a zero." For a while he managed to paint, as he called it, "from spirit," and I remember watching him in the walk-in closet we'd converted into a studio as he closed his eyes, widened his nostrils, and moved backwards through our history to those times when he'd been allowed to stand, without guard or surveillance, on the edge of the Puszta, or the Tisza, or among the hills of the Kárpáts, and engage with the country in the act of "coexistence" that produced his paintings.

The problem was, though, that apart from a few cultivated émigrés willing to buy the paintings he produced shortly after our arrival, nobody really wanted his stuff. The country that he depicted, and the way he depicted it, said nothing to "the philistines," as he called them, who frequented the art markets in Vancouver, Toronto, and Montreal. And, so, as his buyers diminished, my brothers and my mother found ourselves working to support the family, when none of us had ever needed to take a job before; and my father found himself in the position of a man who had once supported his entire family in style, and whose efforts had been solely responsible for the social prestige we enjoyed, now reduced to a guilty, blocked artist, surviving on handouts from his wife and children, who spent all day inside a closet in a cloud of turpentine fumes, staring at a canvas that taunted him so much with its blankness that it was not unusual to come home and find him smoking cigarettes amidst a rubble of broken frames and torn fabric.

Yet, it was around this time—1955 or 1956—that he produced his most successful work to date. I remember that a gallery owner, Heinrich Volker, had been coming around for weeks, trying to convince my father to contribute something to a show he was preparing called Parting the Curtain: Immigrant Art from Eastern Europe. The commission caused substantial disquiet in our home, as my father began viewing it as his "last chance" at breaking into the North American art world; and he began to disclose to us his fantasies about New York and Paris and London—in rambling monologues so out of keeping with his infamous reticence. But as the weeks wore on and Volker's visits became more frequent and insistent, it was clear that my father was getting nowhere with the commission. And we became more and more wary of him, as he now seemed to exist in two states: incessant chatter, or a moody silence that occasionally preceded fits of violence, especially if he was disturbed at work, when he would hurl paint, or a chair, across the room, or bring down a canvas against the edge of a table or door frame. Finally, on the last day possible, with the deadline extended as far as it could go, Volker came to collect the painting. My father was laughing when he walked in, but it was not like any laugh I'd heard, or have heard since, one neither of joy nor delight, but of absolute despair; it was a laughter forced upwards from the pit of the stomach, and so difficult to maintain that it brought tears to my father's eyes.

Volker sat down at the table, wondering, like the rest of us, what had happened to my father, and then seemed to relax a little when he was presented with a canvas wrapped in brown paper. "May I open it?" he asked. "By all means," my father replied. But when the paper came off it, Volker only stared up at us. Apart from my father's signature in the bottom right corner, the canvas seemed, at first sight, completely blank; looking closer, however, we noticed that it wasn't blank at all, but thick, *centimeters thick*, with coat upon coat of white paint. Volker looked at my father in complete wonderment. "I call it *Landscape with Immigrant*," my father said. Then, abruptly, he strode out of the room and back into his closet.

Well, the painting *did*, albeit briefly, put György Ferenc on the map. Remember, this was 1956, when you could still play tricks like that and appear profound. The *Toronto Star* called it "a significant attempt to depict the stalemate resulting from a desire to paint in the midst of an entirely alien subject matter." Likewise, a columnist for *Western Art* wrote, "Of all the paintings on display at Parting the Curtain, none stands out more, for originality or statement, than György Ferenc's *Landscape with Immigrant*, whose uniform white nonetheless betrays its emphasis on the contextual, as the viewer is treated to different shades of feeling depending on the angle at which he is situated in relation to the painting; indeed, the drama of the painting derives entirely from the viewer's perspective, which opens onto vague shadows, the barest detail of brushstroke, and which makes him empathize with the inertia of the immigrant, who, like the painting under our gaze, is cut off from culture, from history, from the country itself, and subject to the minutest of inspections by a culture to which he cannot conform."

None of this meant anything to my father. In fact, all it did was confirm his rapidly mounting disdain for Canadian culture. "The painting was a joke!" he yelled, pounding his fist on the kitchen table. "A complete farce!" And despite Volker's continuous attempts to engage him a second time, my father never again painted anything for an official gallery—at least not willingly.

That doesn't mean he stopped painting. On the contrary, he seemed to sink more deeply into it, though he was now working in complete isolation from the art world—neither speaking to dealers nor fans nor other painters, nor engaging with the diminishing trickle of letters arriving from former students and peers in Hungary—and growing increasingly mystical, explaining himself through remarks we came to expect even before he spoke them: "There is no longer any distraction between the paint and myself," or, "To produce without regard for audience is true art."

And on the weekends he would take us on five- to ten-mile hikes, myself and my two brothers carrying his paints and canvases and easels on our backs while he consulted a surveyor's map and aimed his compass in the direction of the place—the river, the rocky outcrop, the alpine meadow—that might finally speak to him. We would hike for hours, less out of paternal coercion—I was well into my twenties by this time, and Péter was nineteen, and Ákos was sixteen, all big men compared to my slight and delicate father—than out of concern (especially Ákos), wanting to make sure the old man didn't fall off a cliff, or break a leg while moving through underbrush, or get mauled by a bear, and because we desperately wanted him to achieve what he was after, to find some reconciliation with a geography he had no choice but to inhabit. If only he could paint it, we thought, our father would return to being the confident, intense person he'd been in Budapest.

But our father became more and more withdrawn into his labours. And on those weekends, the three of us would sit whispering quietly or wander off from where he was working—to pick berries, get a better view, hunt for grouse—trying to keep ourselves occupied until the sun sank so far in the west we had to rush home to avoid being caught in the woods at night. My father painted a lot in those days, though they were not especially good paintings, everywhere displaying an unease, an awkwardness, as if the painter had only a glancing interest in his subject matter, as if neither landscape nor painter was willing to risk intimacy. And so everything he produced had a formal quality, the kind of restraint that marks a dinner party of bureaucrats who, even in their nods and smiles, are still intent on etiquette.

Most disturbing, however, were the names he gave these paintings. We went to Jasper one summer, and he produced several semi-abstractions of the Rockies, which he termed his Kárpát Series. He was referring, of course, to the Carpathian mountain ranges around Hungary, and each painting was dated, numbered, and titled as if each image derived from this other locale, which was about as similar to the Rockies as a pond is to an inland sea. The titles only added a final—*a fatal*—twist of bewilderment to an already compromised series of paintings. But nobody spoke to my father about it at the time—nobody mentioned the fact that he

couldn't superimpose Hungary over Canada simply by reproducing place names—our silence owing to the fact that he seemed
quite happy with what he'd produced (though he only ever
showed the works to us), and because we were afraid to bring on
another of those ranting fits that always sent his blood pressure
soaring. We let it go.

We let it go for a while. And, then, one day around 1961, Ákos
decided that enough paintings had accumulated in the house, and
what our father really needed was "another chance," as he put it, "at
being recognized for the genius he is." It was then, on that quiet
February night when my brothers and myself gathered to have a
few beers at a local restaurant (only Ákos was living at home by
then), that it occurred to me I was the only one who knew how
truly bad the Kárpát Series was, only I who understood that
György Ferenc was no longer the painter he'd once been. As it
turned out, Péter agreed with me, and he argued with Ákos about
the merits of my father's recent efforts, trying to convince him to
call up the patrons and galleries who owned work from Hungary,
to offer these for a retrospective. But Ákos was certain that Father's
recent landscapes deserved a chance, that we failed to see the
"intentional irony" in them, and that they were at least as relevant
as the *Landscape with Immigrant* he'd produced six years earlier.

"Well, okay, even if you are right," said Péter, "how are you going
to convince him to put the paintings on exhibit? You know how
stubborn he is. And, remember, he hated *Landscape with Immigrant*. It was a joke to him."

"I won't tell him," said Ákos, "I'll just put on the show, and when
it's a success, then I'll tell him. He loves those paintings. I know
he does."

That afternoon, as my brothers drove off, I thought of Ákos dif-
ferently from before, as if his plan had opened holes in my memory, the places of the past that I hadn't, for some reason, noticed
him inhabiting, probably because they were so tied in with my
father and the arc of his diminishing glory. But I remembered how

Ákos had always stayed close to my father when he went trekking after landscapes, always at his elbow—like a familiar, a cherub, a tiny muse—nodding and smiling when the old man's eyes sliced down at his son for approval. And, then, farther back, I remembered the year we spent in the Austrian refugee camp, before Canadian immigration decided to take us, when we would go out for similarly long walks in the countryside; and Ákos, still a child then, had to be picked up whenever we came across a rough patch of ground, or a swamp, or when he was just worn out from the miles we'd gone. And I realized, too, that we had done the same thing in Hungary, near Debrecen, on the Puszta, along the banks of the Tisza, with Ákos sitting on my father's shoulders.

I saw them there now, though my mind was suddenly refocused on my younger brother, wondering if some part of Ákos hadn't been left behind in the paintings my father hid under the floor of the converted chicken coop, or lost in the salons of people who'd turned on György Ferenc at the urgings of the new regime, happy to have his paintings but not his friendship; and it seemed to me that Ákos wanted nothing more than to be holding my father by the hand again, moving through the frame, back into those landscapes, because he was the one still living at home, the one forced to watch the old man degenerate by the day, until my father was utterly lost, unable to remember—as he once had with a skill that astonished us all—the funny, corkscrewed branch, the dead snag at the head of the lake, the patch of chanterelle mushrooms, all those markers that spoke to him, providing instructions on how to return home.

Emigration had been fool's gold for both of them. And it had not occurred to me before, perhaps because Ákos had been so small at the time, that someone other than my father had forever lost an important relationship in the flight to Canada. But while the old man had only lost his footing, my little brother had lost his father, and that was to be deprived of what had been, for as long as he could remember, his only magnetic north.

So it was Ákos now, always Ákos, who had to find my father when he became lost; and it was Ákos who would suffer, later, when the old man became so remote, so distant, so disoriented by the twists and turns he'd taken, that Ákos would be unable to get to him, would be left stalled in the midst of an impassable terrain, not close enough to reach our father but close enough to hear him calling for help.

The exhibit took place on May 12, 1962, at Volker's art gallery, named the Volkerplatz, in Toronto. It was an exclusive show, including almost all of my father's work in Canada—certainly all of the recent landscapes he'd painted on trips to the British Columbia interior, the Kárpát Series, the Hortobágy Memories, the Örség triptych—and Volker had signed a contract with Ákos guaranteeing that the show would stay on—good reviews or bad—for at least one full month.

These reviews were not long in coming. Luckily, Ákos knew that my father would not read the papers, that he had sworn off all news printed in English as being biased and British and totally removed from the realm of truth. The reviews were positive. And, again, this was the early 1960s, when irony was coming into its own as the dominant aesthetic, when norms and institutions, especially those of the nation-state, were being challenged, when it was only too fitting to produce a series of canvases that highlighted the disparity, the unbridgeable gap, between the physical geography of a place and the consciousness we impose on it through the act of naming—with all the patriotic bias and blindness this entails. My father's work, according to *The Globe and Mail*, "expresse[d] the arbitrary nature of naming, and critique[d], in particular, the notion of an immanent geography; throughout, [his] canvases address[ed] the hazards of solipsism, the idea of an essential 'country' that somehow exists outside of, and thus objectively informs, the person perceiving it. It [was] also, with the imposition of Hungarian place names over top of what are obviously Canadian geographical formations, very tongue-in-cheek." The other reviews were similarly positive, drawing attention to the work's statement on how we impose meaning on landscape, and the extreme comedy that results. *It was exactly the kind of thing we did not want my father to read.*

And the pictures were selling, even with the overinflated prices Volker was asking ("The more you charge, the more they think they're worth," he told us.) I remember Ákos gleefully calling us up with each day's profit, and talking about how he was going to take our parents on a trip, how he was going to buy the three of them a new house, how he was going to get my father a library's worth of movies showing every square inch of Hungary.

In the end, it was a phone call that did it. Ákos had instructed Mother to keep our father away from the phone, which was easy enough, given that most of the callers were English and that he was increasingly unwilling to speak the language (my mother would have to find out who the caller was, and whether or not he or she spoke Hungarian, before my father would come anywhere near the receiver). She objected to Ákos's plan at first—having seen the effect the Volker exhibit had had on my father—but relented when Ákos reminded her of the money that my father's pictures would fetch, pointing out to her the dimensions of the home they were living in and comparing them to the places we'd once had, back in the days when György Ferenc was still a bankable name in the European art world. It was easy, of course, what with my father's histrionics and depression to forget what the move had done to my mother, and Ákos was well enough aware—still being at home—that she'd been carrying on her own guerilla warfare against the old man, hoping he might come around, might change his attitude toward the sale of his paintings, and relieve her from the decades she'd already put in scrubbing the floors and toilets of other people's homes.

It would be easy to blame her for complicity in what happened next, and to wish that she'd played some part in mitigating my father's reaction toward the exhibit and Ákos, but what could she have done that we couldn't do? Nothing. And while the rest of us were by now free and on our own, she had to continue living with the old man, leaving him in the morning to clean other people's places, and then returning at night to his rage and silences and refusal to do a single thing other than sit impotently in his studio. Though she never said anything, I think that part of her must have been relieved when Ákos finally left, and she had only one fanatic in the household. I don't blame her for hoping there was some- thing more she could get, not only out of my father, but also out of their life in Canada.

The problem was that when *Art in America* called to do a side- bar, my mother was out buying groceries, and I can imagine how disconcerted my father must have been when he was asked how it felt to have finally achieved recognition in North America, to have been hailed by many of the eminent art critics as one of the first expatriate painters to "attack the illusion of the nation-state and a national culture."

We were at the gallery that day, the four of us, mother included, when my father walked in just as Ákos was delivering a lecture on the Hungarian painters who had influenced György Ferenc, the effect emigration had had on the painting, and his decision to "aes- thetically embrace deterritorialization." I remember turning toward the door when I heard the bells jingling, and having to do a double take between the poster showing an outsized photo of my father's face on the wall and my actual father, who was alternating between a scowl and a look of dismay as he moved back and forth between the reporters and the paintings on the wall.

My father was not an especially strong man, though he had a certain force common to obsessive-compulsives; that is to say, when he wanted something, or when there was a goal to achieve, he had an unlimited energy. And that's how it was that day when he tore through the crowd to where Ákos stood and put his hand over the microphone. There was a momentary hush when we saw my brother's shocked expression, and then, before anyone could intervene, my father swung the back of his hand across Ákos's face, striking him much harder than I'd ever seen him strike anyone (and he had never been one for physical punishment, always preferring the threat of a spanking to the actual task of carrying it out). I was close enough by then, along with Péter, to be able to grab my father and pull him away, and to hear his whisper directed at Ákos, delivered in a Hungarian so thick with hurt that each word was heavy, layered, outlined in black: "From this day you are silent to me, nameless; you do not breathe; you are invisible." And with that, my father shrugged off our hands and walked out of the Volkerplatz.

Ákos was banished from the family; the most loyal son of all, the one most true to the past and to my father's fanaticism, the one who wanted only to please, to make things the way they had been, was cast out into Canada, which to him and my father signified a dead zone where nothing lived, from which nothing emerged—no colours, no forms, no signals of any kind—a rot in the midst of space. Ákos entered my father's Canada that day in the Volkerplatz, straight into the oblivion of exile, from which he has never fully emerged.

He hung around for several months, trying to work himself back into Father's favour, even going so far as to buy back all the paintings that were sold, and sending lengthy letters to the editors of the publications that had responded to the exhibit, explaining that the show had proceeded without "György Ferenc's authorization," and that it was a "crime against the aesthetic intentions embodied in Ferenc's work." But none of it mattered, since my father, despite all of Ákos's protestations, had now entered the lexicon as a foremost painter of the "acultural," as a "satirist of nationhood." I know from my mother that when news of the exhibit finally filtered into Hungary my father began receiving denunciations from the few allies still living there, not to mention the outrage spewed in his direction by a Hungarian immigrant community who were counting, in a sense, on his continued "artistic silence" as a statement on the violation of the "spirit of Hungary" by the Soviets, on their censoring of the "true Hungarian voice." And, so, during most of those days, both Ákos and my father were engaged in similar letter-writing campaigns, trying to explain away the Volkerplatz incident. I have since seen several letters written by my father during that period and, to his credit, he never blames anything on Ákos. In fact, he never even mentions his son, only saying that the paintings were the "signature of despair," fragments of a "failed attempt" to "realize Hungary" from a place where such a realization was impossible.

Ákos was not received back into the family. Naturally, Péter and I continued to see him, even putting him up while he went looking for work and a way back into my father's graces. My mother was equally ineffective in talking her husband out of his decision. She said that he would only look at her when she mentioned Ákos, as one would look at an amnesiac, or at a mole blinded by sunlight struggling across a carpet too thick for its legs, staring at her while she spoke, and then, when she'd finished, shaking his head as if he'd been daydreaming and needed to refocus his attention. When Ákos showed up, my father would disappear into his studio; and if Ákos was still there when he came out, he would move through the room until he could no longer avoid his son, at which point he would stop, stand face to face with the boy and stare not into his eyes but through them, right through the back of Ákos's head, until my brother emptied himself of every apology he could think up, and left.

Eventually, Ákos simply disappeared. He'd been staying at the house my wife and I owned in Cabbagetown, living rent-free in the basement. One morning I realized I hadn't seen him the previous day, that he hadn't, as usual, come up to eat dinner with us, and went downstairs to find that his closet had been cleaned out, that he'd packed up, leaving only a short note: "Dear Gergő, Sorry to leave without saying goodbye, but it didn't feel right when I practised saying it. I have been wondering, lately, if there isn't something out there, some gift, that I might bring to Father so that he will forgive me, and have stepped out to look for it."

I kept this note with me for years, showing it to my father, who acted as if it were an alien hieroglyph, and then perusing it myself, rather obsessively, trying to figure out what "gift" Ákos had gone in search of. It was only after many readings, when the note had become burned into my memory, that I decided the gift was actually a piece of Canada, some fragment that would keep its meaning in the transition from Ákos to my father. He had gone into that whiteness, willingly allowed himself to be swallowed by it, in the hope that he might come across something—a shadow, a glob of colour, a groove of brushstrokes, irony and comedy themselves—that our father could fasten onto, that would help him get a fix on the geography.

In 1967, at the age of eighty, my father died of an aneurysm. In the last few years of his life he had entered the seemingly happiest phase of his artistic career in Canada, leaving the house every morning with easel and paints, off on another excursion into the wilderness, to return home at the end of the day with the canvas still blank, completely untouched, stacking this with the others in his closet as if it were completed, part of a larger body of finished work, then starting off the next morning with a fresh frame and canvas. And we began to see some possibility here, an ultimate statement on the immigrant condition; but when asked about this "work," my father again insisted that these canvases were for "no one," and that he would never consent to show them, no matter how strong a "conceptual statement" we thought they made. He would point his finger at each of us in turn, and lay down the law: "Understand: these paintings are *never* to be exhibited, for one simple reason—" and here he'd smile—"*because they are not paintings.*"

Whatever his opinion, these were, I think, the only works he produced in Canada that came close to satisfying him. Péter and I have each kept one of these canvases, as mementoes.

The old man lay in state for two or three days while the lawyers and my mother went through the papers, coming upon the evolution of Father's will in the notebooks and journals kept in the studio. He'd drafted one or two wills a year, as it turned out, always altering what he wanted done with his remains and paintings and possessions, in a way that reflected his growing alienation in Canada. At first he wanted his effects to come to us, and expressed no particular wish regarding his remains; then, gradually, he went over to wanting his effects donated to the Hungarian Cultural Association, and his body buried in the local Hungarian Calvinist cemetery; and, finally, he wanted everything destroyed, including his body, though he did not specify what we should do with the remnants of this destruction. The three of us decided that his body should be cremated and placed in an urn until such time as the Hungarian government granted us amnesty (they had prevented us, on pain of arrest, from ever returning), and his ashes could be removed to our homeland and scattered in the waters of his beloved Tisza.

(At the same time, there was an emphasis to that final version of the will, not only in the many exclamation points, but also in the thick brush and black paint, dark as India ink, he'd used to slap it down, as if fearing that anything but the boldest manifesto would leave his thoughts open to interpretation. And due to this I felt, disquietingly, that my father, by the time of his death, wanted it made clear that he had gone beyond caring about Canada or Hungary or himself, that he'd reconciled with the great emptiness he'd spent the last half of his life hounding, as if the country had finally opened its mouth to him, and, in doing so, deprived him of his own desire to speak, of his need for anything but silence and an empty mirror.)

As this was 1967, a year thick with Cold War paranoia, we made our decision regarding his remains with the same grim uncertainty with which we'd greeted most of his paintings. There was no reason to hope that our family would ever be granted amnesty to return to Hungary, or that the regime there would topple. We argued—my mother, Péter, and myself—for days over how to manage the ashes, all of us uncomfortable with the fact that a man who had based his whole life on a mystical communion with landscape would now find his remains resting in some ceramic urn, on a mantelpiece, distanced from the earth. In the end, I think we were all afraid that the urn would always be there, reminding us of how unhappy father had been, of how his madness had progressed, and, most of all, of the fact that all his misery had resulted from the fact that he'd wanted the best for us, that he would have endured even the chicken coop as long as it meant he could stay in Hungary, except that he had a wife and sons whose individual futures, for as long as they remained under Soviet rule, would be sorely limited. None of us needed to be reminded of that. And so we dithered.

But by the day of the cremation, it was my mother who'd made the decision to rent a drawer in a crematorium, someplace we could store my father until that day, if it ever came, when he'd return home. It was exactly the kind of compromise my father would have refused, though we put this thought out of our heads because it was convenient, and seemed to accord, however imperfectly, with what we *all* wanted.

It was on that day, some five years after disappearing, that Ákos turned up. We were standing in the cemetery with the priest, clad in the usual funerary black, when my little brother marched in, interrupted the last rites, and picked up the urn from under our noses. He glared at us—shocked as we were by the return of the one person in our family, other than my father, who insisted that every act should be made in consideration of fidelity—spun on his heels and carried the remains out of the graveyard.

We found him later that day, barricaded behind the door to my father's studio. Mother was the first to demand that he come out and explain himself. But Ákos only returned a tirade in which he accused all of us of being untrue to Father's wishes, of being contaminated by a faithlessness that only he, and Father, had had the character to resist, of rejecting our responsibility to the truth for a flimsy compromise. He accused us of being "Canadian." We begged him to come out. But nothing worked.

And when Péter and I finally reached the point of breaking down the door, we found that most of the paintings and journals had disappeared, that the back window was open, and that Ákos and the urn were gone.

I did not see my brother again until 1975, when the government finally rescinded the arrest warrant issued for our family back in the 1950s, meaning we were now free to return to Hungary. He showed up around dinnertime, a week or so after the announcement, just as I was discussing plans for a visit with my wife and kids.

I'm not sure how I recognized him, given that he'd become thinner than anyone I'd ever seen, and that his hair had, for some reason, gone completely white, and was missing in patches and elsewhere sticking straight up in the air, and that his skin, once deep brown, seemed translucent now. Clutched to his chest was the urn.

"Hello, Gergö," he said, in an English that was, if anything, even more warped by Hungarian than ever (and Ákos had been a young boy when we'd arrived in Canada, meaning that he, more than anyone in the family, should have by now completely shrugged off the accent). "I've come to ask you to take Father back to Hungary. If that's okay with you." He sounded sarcastic.

And so Ákos stepped back into our lives. As I guided him to our kitchen table, and pulled over an extra seat, and shovelled a heap of food onto his plate (potatoes and roast and salad that I knew he was too thin to eat but which I offered anyhow to assuage my guilt), I felt that Ákos had in fact gone nowhere in the last few years, that he'd wandered into that blankness my father had always seen and, not finding any sustenance there, had somehow eked out survival on memory alone, on a desire for forgiveness in my father's eyes, while searching for that particle of truth beside which György Ferenc's ashes could rest in peace. Now he'd returned, bearing the marks of that impossible quest. He didn't eat a thing, but merely asked that we boil for him a bit of *erő leves*, beef soup stock. We watched him sip it carefully, holding the bowl with one hand, and balancing the urn on his hip with the other.

We spent much of that night talking about where he'd been, but I was not able to understand much of what Ákos said because he spoke of his travels not in geographical terms—not with the names of cities, towns, forests, lakes, mountain ranges—but in a lexicon so particular, so personal, that I was soon lost, unable to get past the peculiar trees he described, that had led him to a lake tinted a shade of aqua never before seen, from there to a town where people were boarding up houses and moving away, to a description of a city that had within it a building made entirely of "nonreflective glass," and on and on, charting his travels in terms so utterly dependent on the fork in the road he'd chosen, on impressions provided by intersections of weather, people, and times of day, that I soon felt as if he was walking far ahead of me, and that the distance between us was growing with every word.

It would have been different if he'd said Vancouver, or Medicine Hat, or Thunder Bay, or Halifax. And I guessed that his reluctance to use proper names in describing his travels was because he was trying to elude Canada, his motions across the country enacting a ritual dance that might call into being an entirely different geography. Ákos had been wandering Canada in search of Hungary— not his actual home but rather the condition of being, *the possibility*, of home—looking for the law that would somehow, incredibly, let him establish the familiar in the midst of the alien, which would allow him access to the same proportion of awe and reverence and locatedness he had felt in the Puszta, the Kárpáts, or the Felvidék. That he had returned to me suggested how impossible it had been.

He kept the urn, thick with the dirt of his fingerprints, in his hands at all times. And when I asked how he'd lived, he answered vaguely, and I guessed he'd had work here and there, and handouts, and had at other times simply gone without.

It was three in the morning, long after my wife and children had gone to bed, when he asked, "Will you take Father home?"

I looked over at him, refilled his wineglass, and nodded.

Ákos bowed his head and whispered, "Thank you." And when he looked up again his face was full of the exhaustion of the last years. "I've been trying for so long to get him back there."

And so he was there that day the extended family gathered at the airport—Péter and his wife and children, along with my mother—to see us off. Ákos was wearing an old coat that had belonged to my father (he'd come back to Toronto with only what was on his back, and I remember feeling perplexed when I first invited him inside my house, scanning for the suitcase I thought he'd left on the top step), and holding the urn. We were just about to enter the security zone when Ákos paused in the act of handing the urn across to me, and pulled it back. "I just . . ." he paused, "I just want to say goodbye." And he wandered off to the far side of the airport terminal, near the large glass windows overlooking the calm of perfectly manicured lawns, and marshes, and smooth, clear runways, where there were few or no passengers. As my wife and children had already gone ahead through security and customs, I was waiting impatiently, and when, after ten minutes of him saying farewell to a pile of ash, Ákos didn't respond to my call, I quickly walked over to where he stood and asked what the problem was.

He had the strangest look on his face, one I'd seen elsewhere, though I was unable to place it as he handed the urn over to me.

It was empty.

Somewhere along the line, my father's ashes had either leaked out, or been stolen. I ran a finger inside the urn and couldn't even come up with a flake. For the last five minutes, Ákos had stared into the dark void past the ceramic rim, and now was smiling in a way I hadn't seen since before the Volkerplatz incident.

"Is this some kind of joke?" I asked, irritated that my wife and kids were probably waiting for me near the departure gate while I was having this conversation with someone who, I thought, must have completely lost his mind and dumped my father's ashes into the Humber River or Lake Ontario, and either forgotten about it or set up this situation to irritate us into remembering the dead.

Ákos just smiled, and shook his head.

In a fit of panic and disgust, I left him there, smiling, staring into the urn.

It was only many weeks later, when I'd fully realized what it was to lose a country—after I had gone astray in the streets of a city I thought I knew as well as myself, after I'd seen the growth of apartments on the outskirts of Debrecen, after I'd stepped onto the Hortobágy and been unable to shake the sense of infinite distance between the soles of my shoes and the ground they stood upon—that I remembered where I'd last seen the smile Ákos had worn at the airport. You see, either everything had changed in Hungary, or I had changed, and what was most disquieting about the trip for me was not only that I couldn't stabilize *my* sense of being in the country, but that I couldn't even fix upon the country I was trying to stabilize myself in relation to. The greatest nightmare was that *both* of us had changed—the country and myself—and that we were constantly changing, which made the possibility of us ever connecting again a matter of complete chance, the intersection of two bodies on random flight patterns, ruled by equations so different there was little chance of us resting, even for a second, on the same co-ordinates.

My father had smiled like that once, too. We had been climbing for a full half-day in the Rockies, trying to find a particular canyon a local hunting guide had told us about. It was high summer then, and all four of us were sweating and covered with dirt by the time we reached the summit of the cliff overlooking the canyon. My father was especially intent that day, though he must have realized by the time we came to our destination that there was no way he would have time to even begin the painting before we'd have to turn back. The panorama was unlike anything we'd ever seen—deep walls of stone, a raging river at the bottom, thick stands of evergreen, dry and hot—which was usually a bad thing, since what my father wanted, more than anything, was to find a place that at least felt like he'd seen it before. But, today, instead of shaking his head in disapproval I saw him look down into the canyon and smile, beatifically, as if everything that passed in front of his eyes was regular and necessary and right, and for a second or two I thought, idiotically, that maybe he'd finally come to some kind of compromise with the landscape, that he was beginning to realize his place in it, or that he was willing to meet this new country halfway.

Only now, I realize he had not been looking that way at the landscape at all. What he had been looking at, and what had met with his approval, and caused him to smile, was not the river and mountain and clouds and forest that defined the landscape but the nothing, the great nothing, forced down on their contours—the space that framed and thus determined their distinctiveness. The essence of landscape was a thing he finally achieved by not being able to paint it.

And I would have an opportunity to see that smile again and again after my family and I returned to Canada and to Ákos, who had installed himself in the spare bedroom in our basement, the leaky urn and its non-contents sitting on the shelf over where, every night, he rested his head. I would see it every time my little brother pulled off the cap to look at "our father." For it was this nothing, so similar from country to country, Hungary to Canada, that my father had spent his whole life painting toward, and which was realized every time we opened the urn and saw him pressing up at us with an emptiness that was definitive—a pressure we come up against, and which in turn pushes back at us, like some unsettled boundary, whenever we want a limit to who and what we are. Whenever we want a limit to the places we live.

The Laughing Cat

WE CAME UP with the idea on graduation night 1976. I suppose it was the combination of rye and Cokes and dope and beer, but before I knew it we'd made a vow to get together at the Laughing Cat Delicatessen for at least one hour every Saturday—rain or shine or twelve-hour nightshifts or family commitments notwithstanding—for as long as we were still alive.

Things went pretty smoothly at first. The five of us would carry on from whatever we'd been doing the night before, sometimes walking down to the deli straight out of a speakeasy or party, or waking up in one of our apartments, crawling out of sleeping bags, eating a batch of eggs, toast and bacon, then arriving at the Laughing Cat for the first of many Americanos.

But as the years went by, and most of us became occupied with girlfriends, wives, kids, and dying parents, it became less a question of heading there together than catching up with what everyone had been doing. And I was always there first—fresh from a batch of marking, or a reading list for a course I was designing—waiting on their company.

And, then, in 1986, when Nathan Soames's wife took off with an accountant, and that accountant quit working, forcing Nate to near-bankruptcy with support payments out of his meagre millworker's salary, things got drastic. Ben and Hank asked Joe Mara and me to take Nate aside and tell him the last thing any of us needed was him ruining another Saturday by ranting on about how bitter life was (something we were realizing just fine on our own, thanks). But it was Nate's reaction to this—"Oh, so it's okay for Mara to talk about his 'nervous condition,' or Ben about scamming that insurance settlement, or Thomas about how studying leaves him no time to socialize, but I can't complain about Katie walking out on me?"—that made it clear we were going to need some *rules.*

So it was decided that, One, we were men getting together every Saturday; and therefore, Two, we were not there to discuss "emotional issues," since there were plenty of those back in the homes we were seeking relief from; and hence, Three, it was advisable to limit our conversation to sports, politics, and (as best we could) philosophy—though it soon became clear that what we loved most were Joe Mara's stories.

Mara's entrance into the Laughing Cat on the Saturday of November 26, 1996—the date from which I chart the dissolution of our little group—was typical of how he *always* entered the deli: giving the sense that he'd been standing in the doorway for some time, though not quite visible until the moment you saw him, as if he'd congealed out of the city's smog with a mug of coffee in one hand and a burning cigarette in the other, his once neatly trimmed hair now long and slicked back, eyes jagging from one thing to another as though tracing the flight path of a mosquito.

He'd find our table and drop into a seat sideways, turn his profile to us, then extend his mug to the side while puffing silently on a cigarette (this, despite the fact that Vittorio, the proprietor, had NO SMOKING signs posted everywhere—including one on our table, and one on the wall above it). Eventually, Vittorio or one of his nephews would walk over and fill Mara's mug, shaking their heads at the fact that he never even acknowledged their service with a nod. (They had tried, once or twice, to see how long he could hold that mug extended before being forced to ask for a coffee or lower it, but the other customers had been so disturbed by the sight of Mara sitting there, arm trembling spasmodically as the minutes ticked past, that Vittorio, not wanting to lose any business, finally ran over and filled it.)

"You guys ever heard of Selwyn Hughes?" asked Mara. "Contemporary composer. Post-Stockhausen. Lush orchestral pieces intercut with electronic swoops and skronks?" He waited, looking at us expectantly. "C'mon, the guy took apart the twelve-tone system!"

On any normal Saturday, we would have observed the ritual Mara's storytelling demanded: we would have sat there quietly, not responding at all to the question even if we knew the answer, because the unanswered question was Mara's personal muse. The problem on this day, however, was that Hank Davis had brought along a friend—without first checking with any of us—by the name of Alvin Parker, whom I recognized immediately as a fellow professor of literature, although at the city's other university. Every time he spoke I found myself lowering my eyes, hoping he wouldn't recognize me, or that the guys wouldn't mention my name. "Sure, I know him," Parker said smugly. "Wrote 'The Last Stage of Evaporation.' Wonderful music. He stopped composing—sold his records and disappeared—about ten years back."

It was the first time I'd seen Mara off balance. He retracted his head as far as his neck would let him, then lifted the mug and cigarette in quick succession to the place where his lips used to be, doing this twice before he realized they'd moved a couple of inches south, so that by the time he'd managed a slurp and puff he looked like someone chasing after himself. "Who are you?" he asked. But when Parker offered his handshake, Mara pushed his head even farther back, as if the hand were reaching up to grip his throat. "Parker, huh?" Mara considered the information, peering at him from a long remove.

Everyone shifted in their seats, except for Parker, who looked around ingratiatingly, unaware of what he'd done. With great effort, Mara pulled himself together and did something else I'd never heard him do: he stuttered. "Y-y-y-you know who I saw him with yesterday morning at the corner of Bloor and Ossington?"

"Yo-Yo Ma," said Parker and Mara simultaneously.

The hand holding Mara's cigarette dropped to his side. "What the fuck?" His face was ashen. "H-h-h-how . . . How did you?" And when Parker explained that he'd seen a picture snapped by some paparazzi and buried in the back pages of the weekend Entertainment section of the *Globe*, above a short article on the enigma of Selwyn Hughes, Mara rose from the table and looked around the deli frantically, as though desperate to avoid capture. Already I could see Vittorio and his nephews edging toward our table, ready for trouble. "Did the article say what Hughes and Yo-Yo talked about?" And then Parker—finally realizing he'd broken with some protocol Hank should have warned him about—replied that no, the article had only remarked on Hughes' disappearance from the music scene, and on how rare a sighting of the great composer was, adding quickly, and by way of an attempted apology, that he would now stop interrupting Mara's "delightful picaresque," and be happy just to listen to the "episodic narratives" Mara "inscribed on the streets of Toronto."

"Picaresque?" asked Nate. "What's a picaresque?"

Ignoring the last part of Parker's response, Mara pointed the butt end of his cigarette at him, saying, "I knew it! Only *I've* got the story!" And with that he turned on his heels and rushed for the door, twisting one last time toward us as he hit the top step, saying, "I'll be back soon. Very soon!"

It took a second for what had happened to sink in. Parker turned toward Hank in his seat, hands up in a protestation of innocence. I looked at the door through which Mara had exited, then over at Nathan and Hank and Ben, seeing the same question in their eyes—before Ben finally rose and began shouting at Parker and Hank, which gave Vittorio and his nephews exactly the excuse they needed to jump in and escort us out of the Laughing Cat.

While Vittorio stood on the sidewalk, shaking his finger and reading us the riot act, I saw Nate lean toward Parker and ask again, "What's a picaresque?" When Parker walked off, head bowed, Nate followed, still asking questions.

...

I, of course, walked the other way, not toward home but along the avenues, searching for some sign of Joe Mara through Chinatown and Kensington Market, then Queen Street, before reluctantly boarding a bus outside the Art Gallery of Ontario.

Truth was, I had no way of finding Mara and I knew it, and once I got home that night I reflected with an unwanted nostalgia on where, exactly, the Laughing Cat had brought us. Thinking of the rules we'd devised in the wake of Nathan's divorce—put in place to guarantee that the deli remained impervious to change, that it always afforded the same experience week after week, without the ups and downs, the bewildering flux, that defined life *outside* its walls—it became shockingly apparent that each of us had long ago lost track of what the other guys did in terms of work; whether they were single, married, divorced, remarried, or lonely; how many kids they had. Even the phone numbers we'd once been able to recall by reflex were now lost in the lists of "J. Mara's" and "N. Soames's" and "H. Davis's" and "B. McCormack's" in the phone book, names we couldn't reference against a single known address. For the last ten years, or perhaps fifteen, I had no idea what any of them had been going through. Oh, sure, there were telltale signs—the shaking of hands when Nate reached for his coffee, Mara's increasing abstract-edness, Ben quietly asking one or another of the guys to foot his bill for twelve months on end, the spots of baby food that all of a sudden vanished from Ben's clothing—details I'm sure we'd all noticed, but which had faded into the background, or disappeared altogether when their trials, whatever they were, passed, and they returned to being the people we'd always known. But none of us ever asked what the matter was. It was the rules. And it was the rules I blamed that night, tossing and turning, afraid I'd never see my friends again.

This, as it turned out, was not so unreasonable a fear, because the very next Saturday, Vittorio, upon seeing me enter the deli, ran over to prevent me from sidling up to our table. "You can't meet here anymore," he said, arms folded. I glanced at the front counter and saw his nephews staring at me through the aperture that separated the deli from the kitchen. "I'm fed up with you guys," he said. "With your crazy stories. Shouting and yelling and laughing. Disturbing my customers. And that guy Mara and his cigarettes. Can't he see the signs?" He waved his hands in the air as though I had a cigarette in hand at that very moment and he was fanning the smoke from his face. "It was okay at first," he continued. "You made my place look busy. But now . . ." He dropped a hand onto my shoulder. "I can't afford to give up a table to a bunch of guys who do nothing but order coffee." I scratched my head and looked at the customers, who were looking at me.

By the time I'd made it home—again searching for Mara through the neighbourhoods around Little Italy and downtown, though more frantically than before—I had already figured out what it would take to appease Vittorio. But there was an undertone to my thinking that day, a trace of guilt, for whenever I thought of us getting back together it occurred to me that in listening to Mara we'd actually been doing something *to* him, that our passivity as an audience was in fact an *activity*, and a harmful one at that. And as I punched in the URL for the online menu of the Laughing Cat, and tried to stay undisturbed by the usual silence of my phone, calculating the kind of order we'd have to place to make it worth Vittorio's while, I kept brushing from my mind the sight of Mara standing at the corner of King and Yonge—Mara in his long hair and threadbare clothes, the shoes that looked more like slippers (were they slippers?), the way I would always avoid him while going to work so he couldn't ask where I was headed, the way I couldn't help watching him anyhow, sometimes even following after him, intrigued by the possibilities of his life. Mara was often just standing there, staring up, searching the sky, or leaning against a bank or a lamppost, checking out the passersby, or strolling in a way that showed he had no destination in mind, coffee cup and burning cigarette always in hand, absently waved at and welcomed by the waiters and waitresses of coffee shops and greasy spoons, as if the whole city were his living room. I spent the better part of that day fighting off these memories, as well as those from before: Mara receiving the Principal's Award in high school, giving a speech at his wedding, telling us how quickly he'd risen from clerk to manager—all these memories from the days before our rules came into play, and which I couldn't square with the days that came after except through the saddest of theories.

Finally, it was Nate who kicked me into action, with a phone call. He was silent for a second on the other end, stunned by the speed at which I'd picked up the phone. "Thomas?" he asked. When I responded, he took a deep breath. "Look, I'm sorry to call you at home, but you're the only guy I knew for sure in the phone book." He paused. "Not too many Corvins out there." I laughed in relief, so happy just to hear from him, and he went on as if taking a cue: "We need to figure out the Laughing Cat. And you should be the one to call Vittorio."

"Me? Why me?" I asked.

"Because you're the quiet one. The guy who never talks. He likes that."

"I talk," I said.

"Not much you don't," he replied, "and never to tell stories." I couldn't help but hear a subtext in the statement, as if Nate were envious of my situation, or angry, as though he'd suddenly discovered I'd been withholding something, information that might have helped when he'd really needed it. "You've got no story," he said, his voice so hard it was like a hammer hitting the receiver, and I realized this was the first time in a long time—as long as I could remember—that any of the men from the Laughing Cat had addressed me personally.

Once Nate supplied me with the addresses and phone numbers— excepting those of Mara, who was too well hidden, or too far out of the loop, for Nate's resources—it still took six weeks to settle with Vittorio. Six weeks that started with him hemming and hawing—winding me up for the sum he had in mind—followed by multiple negotiations and renegotiations of what I came to call the "Laughing Cat Contract." Every time Vittorio made a recommendation for our menu one or more of the guys—who were awkward on the phone, as if my calling them, however necessary, constituted a violation of the rules, as if my asking what they'd like to eat and drink at the Laughing Cat made them accessories to a crime—would want something *else*, which I would then have to take back to Vittorio, who'd either reject it or multiply it by five or offer an alternative to. Looking back, it's amazing that we ever managed to reach a consensus: four Americanos, one espresso, two slices of panini, three large pizzas topped with artichoke hearts, feta and anchovies (which nobody liked but which Vittorio insisted on because there'd been a mistake in ordering and he was overstocked), five Oranginas (which nobody liked either, though they were preferable to the Italian cola Vittorio had also overstocked), a basket of focaccia and a plate of balsamic vinegar mixed in olive oil, and, finally, in place of the large cake Vittorio wanted, one platter of Sushi Combo B from Sushi-Ya down the street, which Ludovico ordered in at considerable markup. The total came to about one hundred dollars every Saturday.

As it turned out, it didn't matter, for we only met once more at the Laughing Cat.

Mara was absent that day, and that's all the explanation *I* need for why the event was such a failure. The rest of us were there, as usual, though that's all that was usual, as if the six weeks between Saturdays—the first break of any kind since we'd started meeting twenty years ago—had revealed how alien we were to one another, how our get-togethers had become a ritual emptied of all content. Or maybe it was the food sitting on the table, the coffees and sodas and pizzas and raw fish congealing in the warm air blowing from the overhead vents, reminding us of how artificial the set-up was, how far from the spontaneity of that night twenty years ago when we'd vowed to always meet here. And while none of us said anything, I knew our thoughts were the same, sitting around the table, awkward and halting in our speech, with the exception of Hank and Ben, who were even more awkward, still upset over their argument with one another. Of the five, only Nate and I tried to resurrect the old spirit, with me encouraging everyone to try the food, and Nate warming up to tell one of *his kind* of stories.

Nate's stories were always of a type—filled with blue-collar workers and bars and cars and divorce. While the early stories, predictably, had been about the bitterness of marriages falling apart, and infidelity, always with the man being on the wounded end, as the years went by Nate seemed to be making a conscious effort to switch to the woman's point of view. And though the stories always suggested the woman's ultimate culpability—leaving the five year old in charge of "babysitting" so she could meet with a younger man living down the street; or disappearing from home for three days with a doctor she met at a funeral—over the years a tenderness had crept into the telling, so that when, at the end of the story, the woman looked back over the years, as she invariably did, trying to understand the loss of her moral and intellectual certainties, what I always got—though judging by the reactions of the others I was probably alone in the respect—was a sense of Nate trying to adopt a different attitude, as if to recognize how little he knew about these women was also to remind himself of perspectives other than his own. And what I loved about the stories, truly loved, was Nate's striving for these perspectives in the face of his continual failure to achieve them. For, in the end, what the women of his stories always came to was an acknowledgment of how contradictory our motives are, of how the consequences of choice, in the long run, often turn out to be of no consequence whatsoever—except, of course, in the moment of the decision.

But not everyone, as I said, liked Nate's stories as much as me. And they were not the kind of stories that should have been told that Saturday. What we really needed was Mara, another of his magical adventures, something to make us wonder and laugh and believe anything was possible. And when Nate finished, Ben shook his head and wondered why anyone would bother to tell a story, much less listen to one, where the "high point" is some woman looking back at her life and realizing that the only lesson she can take from it—"which is more of a non-lesson," Ben added—is that "things just happen."

There was a moment of silence during which I could hear the cracking of the cooling pizza crust. Nate stared at the floor and shifted his feet. "It's not really about the woman," he said after a while. "It's about me. But I don't know what the point is," he said, not lifting his head. And, then, after a moment he did lift it: "I bet Alvin Parker could tell us." It was a comment that would have appeared sarcastic only to those who hadn't been sitting with Nate for twenty years. And his face lit up with something like hope, though it only took Hank a moment to respond.

"Forget it," he said.

"But why?" asked Nate. "He could help me . . . help us get out of . . ." He waved his hands around, not so much indicating the world as the room, as if the Laughing Cat was a trap Nate had been struggling to get free of, or transform.

"I don't think you get it," said Hank, standing up. "Alvin was shook up by what happened here. He doesn't want anything more to do with us."

Hank reached for his coat. "I think I have to go now," he said, though he was not referring to this particular Saturday. "It's not so much fun without Mara, is it?" he said, and there was that same guilty undertone to his words as there had been to my thinking about Mara five weeks ago.

"Mara will be back," I yelled, and I was amazed to discover how desperate I was, my language as full of struggle as Nate's. "I think you should stay," I said. "I really do. I mean, we've been meeting for twenty years!" And once I'd begun there was no way of preventing myself from begging. "This is just a lull! Our first one! I mean, we made a vow! You're not going to break it over something as minor as this?"

"Our first lull?" He looked at me. "Where have you been? You know how many times I've driven here wondering why I bother coming? I brought Alvin along to inject some life into this place!"

I stood up. "What are you talking about? You love it here," I said. "It's the only break you get from your wife and kids."

Hank put on his jacket and shook his head. "You're whacked," he murmured. "I don't have any wife and kids. Not anymore." And Hank looked away from me then, though I did not know whether it was because locking eyes would have forced him to vent his anger, or because he couldn't endure the pity it would have inspired. "This hasn't been fun for a long time," he said. And with that he put on his coat and walked out the door. And I would have reached after him, or yelled something, except I caught sight of Vittorio standing in the doorway to the kitchen, arms folded, gazing warily at us, and I found myself standing, hands in fists, caring about Hank's departure to the point of violence.

Within ten minutes we'd paid up and left, and when I got outside I looked both ways, watching the backs of my friends receding down the street, and I wanted to yell at them, to say something to make them turn, though in the end I didn't, partly because they were too far off to hear and partly because I paused, and waited too long, wondering whether maybe, just maybe, they might not recognize my voice at that distance. You see, in all the years we'd been meeting I had never told a story, and thus had never needed to lower my voice to a whisper, or raise it to a shout, or do any of the things required to dramatize an incident. The only voice they'd heard me use was dead-flat, going on about some point of politics or sports, or turning to Vittorio and his nephews to order coffee.

...

I spent the better part of the next two weeks either at work or on the streets, searching for Mara, dreaming up ways to entice him back to the Laughing Cat, thinking that if I could persuade him then everyone else would return as well. It was only when I found him—entirely by accident—that I realized why it had been suddenly so hard to locate a man who'd once been omnipresent downtown and in Little Italy, a man you had to go out of your way to avoid.

Mara was wearing a sweatshirt hood, its strings pulling the fabric so tightly around his face that only the rhythm of coffee mug and cigarette—the one-two, one-two motion with which they disappeared into the darkness shading his face—gave him away. When I approached he jumped.

"Jesus, Thomas," he said. "We can't talk here!" He grabbed my shoulder and pulled me into an alley that ran between buildings, crammed with overflowing crates and dumpsters and the occasional sleeping body.

"Mara, I've been looking for you everywhere."

"Yeah, well, I'm travelling incognito these days." He drained his mug, and then lit a new cigarette off the butt of the old one. "You didn't see Nate out there?"

I shook my head. "We missed you at the Laughing Cat last time," I said.

"Hey, I don't break my vows easily," he replied. "But *he* was there." And when I asked who, he replied, "Nate! Nathan Soames!"

"Mara, what are you talking about?"

And then Mara told me what had been happening over the eight weeks since his last appearance at the Laughing Cat. It seemed Nate had taken to keeping Mara company during his rambles along the streets of Toronto, the two of them chatting away between stops at greasy spoons and coffee shops, the whole thing so natural it took Mara several weeks to realize Nate's "company" was actually a form of *stalking*, at which point, in a moment of panic, he began actively avoiding him, until their game of hide-and-seek grew so desperate Mara turned paranoid, a man in hiding. The worst of it, he said, was his inability to relax, which in turn made it impossible for him to fall into the easy stroll that had been his way on these streets, a lolly-gagging shuffle that was less an activity than a way of insulating himself from the environment, less a motion than a *home*. And this walk, Mara admitted, its *ease*, was what had always led him to the stories he recounted at the Laughing Cat.

"It's really terrible, Thomas," said Mara. "I used to run into the most amazing people. And I'm not just talking eccentrics," he said, waggling a finger in my face. "Composers, politicians, actors, you name it. But now, ever since Nate's been following me around, well . . . you'd be amazed at the *ordinariness* of that guy's life!" And Mara recounted to me the days and weeks they'd spent together, following commuters with birthmarks, twitches, inappropriate clothing, details that had once led Mara to stories, but which now led them nowhere: to corporate buildings, ferny lobbies, the bland hiss of elevators going up and down. Nothing ever happened, and for the first time Mara understood what it was like to live in Nate's world, a place empty of magic, where the ticks and nuances of men and women were indicators only of malaise and desperation, where it seemed as if the city's streets and buildings, because they determined the routes and spaces available to commuters also determined their stories. It was the same story, over and over, and totally unlike the tales Mara had come upon up to now—incidents so rare they seemed to operate against the odds by which we meas-ured the ordinary.

"I don't know a lot," said Mara. "No, no, no," he shook his head so frantically. "But I know this: I would not want my life to look anything like the story Nate's living. And I'm getting out of his trap!" He poked me in the chest as he spoke this last bit of sen-tence, then peeked out of the alley, and quickly stormed off.

Despite the fact that I had taken Mara's hint on "stalking" him, and resolutely avoided setting foot anywhere in downtown or Little

Italy, I still found my eyes wandering to the windows of taxicabs and streetcars, hoping I'd see him standing beside an accident involving a taxi and a stretch limousine, his hand on his chin as he negotiated a truce between a cabbie and a deposed king, or something equally unlikely. I wanted to see Mara back in the scenes he'd described to us at the Laughing Cat. And every time I had to force my face from the window, I would be disturbed by the thought that it was not Mara's walk but rather his *stories* that had insulated him from the city, and from *himself*, from the fact that sometime during the last twenty years he'd gone crazy.

At night I sat in front of my stack of papers, the books on the shelves crowding around like a tomb of paper, portals to worlds I was barred from, to which entry demanded my transformation into ink. It never occurred to me, even then, that maybe Nate was experiencing similar difficulties, but from the other side, from *within* the story—desperate for an exit from the plot, from his status as a character.

The sad part, of course, is that knowing this still wouldn't have made me contact Nate had Alvin Parker not called first. "This is Thomas Corvin?" he asked, a few nights after my meeting with Mara. "*Professor* Thomas Corvin? Seventeen peer-reviewed articles in the MLA bibliography? Two books? Tenured in the Department of English at the University of Toronto? That's you, isn't it?"

There was such accusation in his voice that it emerged from the phone more as a physical presence than a sound, and it took me a second, even after I'd figured out who was calling me, to find the courage to respond. When I told him yes, it was me, Parker's voice grew even angrier, as if my admission should have come earlier, *two months earlier*, when he was wilting under Ben's rage. "Don't worry," he said, "your secret's safe with me." I waited a moment to respond to this because Parker's breath seemed withheld, on the verge of adding something further, but in the end I heard nothing except a soft click, perhaps the sound of a wristwatch tapping on the receiver, or an open mouth that, wanting to say more but not knowing what, had shut with a quiet setting of teeth. And I realized right then that Alvin Parker, beyond the revealing or safeguarding of my secret—that I was an academic—had, like me, *nothing to say*, and that he had understood this in the instant of Ben's reaction, when it was made clear that being a literary critic was an occupation best kept hidden in the company of men telling stories.

When Parker spoke again, it was not about me, but Nate. "Your friend—*Soames*—he's been calling me constantly the last three weeks. I'm getting scared to pick up the receiver."

This time, it was Parker's turn to wait for a response, because I had taken a breath, but no words were forthcoming. Parker laughed. "You know what? He wanted to know if he could take one of my courses! Especially interested in metafiction, he tells me." Parker laughed again. "When he speaks about it it's like listening to a man making his last confession. There's this spiritual aspect to what he's saying, *this faith*. Like he believes that by thinking about stories from the outside he'll be able to get outside his shitty life." There was another spot of silence, then more clicking, and I realized Parker was not setting his teeth but grinding them. "I thought you should know because he sounds more and more disturbed all the time."

"What did you tell him?" I asked, scanning the room for my coat and keys, wanting to depart for Nate's place even before getting off the phone with Parker.

"I said," Parker whispered, "that he could have my knowledge, *all of it*, for what it's worth. In return, I'll take his story. I also told him there's nothing worse than the kind of escape he's dreaming of. *It's no escape at all.*"

I nodded into the receiver, resisting the urge to turn my back to the books still leering at me from the shelves.

"I want you," said Parker, by way of finalizing our conversation, "to get him to stop calling me."

"Okay," I said, though what I really wanted was to tell Parker to fuck off.

...

It has always been my belief—though this is something I don't advertise too widely in the department where I work—that the whole purpose of art, the very reason for embarking on it in the first place, is *to entertain us*, and, by entertaining, to make us *forget*. For there is always a story prior to the stories given to us to tell, and this is the desire to tell, to put experience into the best possible form, the one that will make other people gather around, rapt with attention. This was why we were at the Laughing Cat in the first place, as if a wooden table at some average delicatessen could serve as a fire for us to gather around, warping hardship into something that made us laugh, or nod, or consider, and whether the stories were based in fact or imagination didn't make the telling of them any less an art. It was art, not truth, we came for.

Which meant that if you really wanted to forget, really get outside of yourself, then what you needed was not to talk *about* stories, as Nate wanted to do, but to listen *to* them, or, better still, tell them, and not in a repetitive way, but in an attempt to breach what little we knew, and the forms in which we knew it. And that's why I had remained silent about what I did for a living, and why we had developed the rules that safeguarded our forgetting.

It was with this in mind that I drove to Nate's that night. Though I now realize there was also an element of guilt there—that for all the years we'd been regularly dosing ourselves with the medicine of stories, we'd also been letting friends like Mara and Nate spin out of reach, entertaining ourselves with the wonderful tales that to someone else might have been evidence of their decline and of the imperative to help them. We'd warmed ourselves in the heat and light of two men burning out.

By the time I tracked down Nate's address among the contacts he'd supplied when we were trying to resurrect our group, and found it on a map, and driven over to his place, it was well past sunset, and I had to drive slowly through the trailer park, threading between abandoned wagons and tricycles, slowing down for speed bumps that, being unpainted, were invisible in the dark. I recognized the trailer next to Nate's, a rectangular box painted over to look like a case of Molson Canadian. He'd told an anecdote about this once—one of the few that were funny—how the guy had run out of money halfway through and had gotten Molson to sponsor him for the rest of the paint, only to spend the money on beer.

I knocked on the door, but found it open, and the force of my knuckles pushed it further ajar. Peeking in, I saw the flicker of a television, and then Nate, who was sitting on the couch with a bottle cradled between his legs, licking his lips absently and staring at the ceiling as though deciding on whether to let in whoever was at the door.

"Nate?" I said, quietly. His head snapped into place, the look in his eyes one of surprise. "Can I come in?" I asked. He shook his head. I looked around uncertainly, as though the lack of invitation was not due to me but the door I'd chosen, as though trying a different one, or a window, might elicit a different response. "I spoke with Alvin Parker," I said.

Nate raised the bottle to his lips. "I've been reading some," he said, and I was surprised to hear his voice so clear and lucid, not drunk at all. "I read one—it was pretty complex though—which said the forms of our stories are also the ones through which we process our experiences, and, as a result, how we think of the world and our place in it." Nate was speaking slowly, reciting sentences he'd memorized, and I had to lean my head through the door to hear. "Neat argument, eh? It's like the structures . . . the stories our parents give us are already making us think of the world in certain ways before we even get *into* it." I wanted to tell him that if you traced things back you'd find the world came first, then the stories, or that the things that happened in the world and the stories were so intertwined you couldn't separate what came first from what came after.

But Nate continued before I'd had a chance to speak. "When Katie left it was weird." He took another drink. "I'd be walking around places and what I was seeing, instead of actual things, was how she *wasn't there*." He glanced in my direction. "Now how can that be? Tell me. How in the name of God can you see something that isn't there? Is that even possible, or did I go crazy?" He waved his hand over a shoulder to suggest the past, and I could hear his nails scratching the wall behind the couch he sat on. "Nothing connected, you know? It was like her absence was also the absence of whatever it is that makes things connect. And that's why this book is so interesting. It tells me that the way we connect stuff—like the past to the present, or ourselves to other people, to *things* see?—is through 'meaning.' We're able to make meaning when we can draw a line that binds stuff together. And that's what a story is, I guess." He tilted the bottle between his legs, reading the label, and then, holding it by the neck, placed it on the coffee table in front of him. "The weird thing is," he whispered, ". . . is that all these years, down at the Laughing Cat, my stories have been doing the opposite thing: they've been about how things *don't connect*. I thought I was coming to grips with that—making peace with a world that doesn't mean, but just *is*."

He coughed. "I've been trying to figure out why I keep doing it, you know? Why keep sending Katie the money? I know that guy she's with isn't working. I know the kids don't see all of what I send them, that she shovels some of it his way. Why do I do it?" He looked around at the trailer. "I mean, who needs this? I could just disappear. Lot's of men do it, you know. They just walk out. Slip from one life into another. That's what Mara reminded me of every week," he folded his hands into the place where the bottle had been. "I mean, Mara doesn't live in the world at all! It's like he's a ghost or something, slipping in and out of himself. And I'd listen to his stories, that incredible life he's living, and I'd think: why can't I do that? Why am I stuck here, making these payments, forcing myself to live in this . . . shithole."

He opened the hands in his lap and looked at the palms. "All these years I've been trying to explain—mainly to myself—why I do what I do, what makes me choose this, and the more time goes by the less I can come up with a story that makes sense." He laughed bitterly. "All I come up with are stories about how you've got to accept the fact that you do things, make choices, that don't always make sense."

My neck was becoming stiff with the weight of holding my head through the door. "I've been trying really hard not to blame her for this. Really," said Nate. "And then that guy Parker comes to the Laughing Cat, and starts talking about Mara's stories, and I feel like maybe I have a chance again." He looked hard at me. "But we all know how that worked out. Either I'm beyond help, or nothing ever happens on Mara's walks and he's totally crazy." Nate trained his gaze on me now, as though nothing existed but the next question: "Why didn't you, though?"

"Why didn't I what?" I asked, withdrawing my head through the crack, scared that it presented too much of a target.

"Help me," he shouted. "When I could still be helped!" He'd risen suddenly off the couch and come to the door. "You knew all about this stuff. You were on the outside the whole time! And you were just sitting there, listening to me struggling along. And you stayed quiet. Why didn't you help me when you had the chance?" I looked at him. "Even just being able to sit in silence, like you do, even that would have been better than this!"

His face was straining out of the crack in the door now, his mouth so wide it looked as if his teeth were projecting from his face. I stepped back. "Nate," I said, shocked, "that book you've been reading . . . it's just another story."

He pushed me with full force, toppling me backwards and down the three steps that led to his deck. "Don't patronize me!" he shouted.

I stood up, my pants covered in mud. "Nate," I tried to sound earnest, "the reason I didn't say anything is not because I'm keeping it secret. I haven't got anything to tell you! What?" I threw up my hands. "You think I could take you out? Take you *where?* Silence isn't a place; it's nothing, Nate. The reason I haven't talked about it is because you *can't* talk about it. That's what silence—*real silence*—is." I paused and lowered my arm, and then said quietly, "Nobody's ever really outside, Nate. We're always stuck in the beginning." And I wanted to add something more, a qualifier, words that would give Nate a sense of how lucky he was, how he had managed, in telling his stories, at least to sit at the Laughing Cat and have us listen, to take us away from what we were thinking about, even if what he said was sad, even if all he accomplished was testifying to himself—a man who would not acquiesce to defeat, to abandonment, who'd rise every morning and start all over again, formulating his next story as if just being able to speak was redemption in itself.

My problem, I reflected, opening my mouth to speak, then closing it as Nate stepped to the top of the stairs, was that I wanted so much to tell, and couldn't begin, that the instant I thought of one particular story another hundred would crowd it out, pointing to its limits and politics. But every time I wanted to speak of a man who couldn't make up his mind, who'd prevented himself from making the basic gesture of commitment to others, whose sum total of company took place once a week at the Laughing Cat, all I could do was think of *how it could be said.* And that, dear Nate, I wanted to say, is all of my story.

Nate just stood above me, glaring down with his fists hanging to either hip, a scowl of betrayal on his face.

And in the days since I threaded my car back through the tricycles and wagons and trash, and the days since I once again started catching sight of Mara downtown, I have gone over and over what I should have said, how I should have begun, all the variations that might have made Nate open his ears to me, that would have made at least part of what we had at the Laughing Cat once again possible. I have weighed the options while the books crowded upon me, a massing of that terrible knowledge that always makes me step backward when I think I'm stepping forward. The knowledge that spares me no room to speak.

Philip's Killer Hat

BEFORE I GET INTO THIS BUSINESS about my brother, Philip, I should probably say a word or two about the fez. Not the historical fez, mind you—the hat invented in the Moroccan city of the same name in the ninth century; the one Mahmut II made the official headgear of the Ottoman Empire from 1826 until 1925, when Atatürk, "the great reformer," outlawed it in favour of the Panama hat—but rather the one worn by Thelonious Monk in the CD booklet of the recording, *Monk Alone*.

Philip was certain that a careful examination of the pictures in which Monk is wearing the fez revealed the tightness of its fit. He'd draw my attention to the picture in which the hat seems to be pulling the meat of Monk's face upward, distending the pianist's mouth in a painful sneer. Might it not be possible, Philip wanted to know, that Monk's hats were all too small for him, and had maybe, through the action of "squeezing the plates of his skull," contributed to the madness that overtook the jazz musician and possibly resulted in his early retirement and death?

Philip had drafted several letters on this theme, all addressed to the beneficiaries of Monk's estate. Luckily, he always needed my editing skills, and so I found myself, every other week, trying to dissuade him from sending them. "Think of the conclusions they might draw," I said, getting him to imagine how outraged they'd be to hear Monk's struggles explained as nothing more than the result of ill-fitting hats. "Or think," I said, "how their own imaginations might get carried away." I told him they might attribute Monk's taste for too-tight hats to some kind of death wish, the pianist's desire to slowly drive himself insane. "Or even worse," I said, "what if they think the hats were made too small *after the fact?*" And I could see Philip tremble at the thought of Monk's relatives looking with suspicion at one another, at the staff, at the musicians who'd kept Monk company, wondering who had shrunk the hats that had destroyed the pianist's mind. Our meetings always ended with him ripping up the letter and promising to redraft it to prevent any possible offence. "Good idea," I would say, letting out a sigh of relief, and watching him walk back down the stairs into the basement. But even when my objections seemed to anger him, even when I could see him struggling to contain his disappointment, there was always a touch of gratitude to Philip's response, as if my words had given him a blissful reprieve from the obsession that would, within a few hours, overtake him once again.

It wasn't long before Philip was coming home from the library with stacks and stacks of books—all of them about hats. By this point he'd had the pictures of Monk blown up so that he could tack them on his wall and cover them with notations and measurements and various mathematical formulas, all in his cramped shorthand. I'd be down there changing the sheets on the bed or cleaning out the cupboards or vacuuming, and would have to constantly run back from what I was *really* doing—trying to decipher what he'd written—to what I was *supposed* to be doing, whenever I thought I heard the doorknob turn, or Philip returning up the driveway with another armful of books.

Eventually, he brought to me the report he'd written. There was a long preface, filled with innumerable citations, in which he elaborated upon what he called the "killer hats of history." Included was the infamous "Harley-Davidson Cap," identified by numerous coroners as the primary cause of a dozen or more fatal vehicle accidents, having been inherited by a series of motorcyclists (all related by blood), whose eyes it had fallen over (or so went the coroners' reports) just at those moments when they should have been paying attention. Included was the picture of an iron hat shaped like a colander that the "Mesopotamians" (according to Philip) would heat until it was red hot, then force down upon the skull of the victim, the tiny holes permitting the escape of the steam and smoke of burning scalp. He also wrote of something dubbed "Lincoln's Top Hat," that had been worn first by two innocents and then a succession of twelve foolhardy men, all of whom believed they could prove themselves the favoured sons of fate by not being shot, while wearing it, outside a theatre. Finally, there was the anecdote about the ten-gallon hat owned by the famous football coach, Lefty Franzen, in which he was found dead one night outside a notorious Detroit gay bar, the hat having been forced down on his head until he suffocated. As a result of his horrific murder, Lefty's wife, Abigail, decided to ignore the explicit instructions left in her husband's will, and left the hat out of his coffin. But this proved a grievous mistake, since three years later Abigail was found dead in her apartment, the result of a violent burglary where the only thing stolen was the cowboy hat. "It is said," wrote Philip in his preface, "that Lefty's murderer, frightened by the DNA testing recently introduced into police procedure, wanted to ensure that traces of his skin and hair could not be recovered from the hat."

The bulk of Philip's manuscript, however, was taken up with a laboured discussion of Thelonious Monk's skull: extrapolations taken from photos blown up to scale, projections of yearly shrinkage rates for the fabrics out of which were made the pork-pies, fezzes, bowlers, berets, toques, cavalry caps, and other hats Monk had worn (or at least those available from photographs). The report ended with a request to be given access to the various measurements of Monk's head, from adolescence to death, and to his remaining hats.

I read the entire manuscript two or three times over, asking Philip to give me several days with it, and went through the mistakes in spelling and punctuation and pronoun agreement and modal verbs, and then gave it back to him for corrections, saying there was no way Monk's estate would take him seriously if it wasn't 100 percent grammatically perfect. I thought it would take him two weeks, if not three, to make the changes, but there he was the following afternoon with "the final draft." A few days later, when he asked what I thought, I replied that it was clean and perfect and that under normal circumstances I would recommend he send it, except I wondered whether it might tip off the family to the importance of the hats, and whether they wouldn't be inclined, in that case, to investigate the matter with their own scholars and doctors, or, worse, in the event that it implicated them in Monk's "murder," destroy the hats altogether. Philip held the manuscript for a while and then his shoulders slumped and he turned and went down the stairs, closing the door softly behind himself. I swore I heard a whispered "Thank you" as he went.

And when our sister, Lucia, asked how Philip was doing I would tell her how tiring it was to disappoint him all the time, and that I was beginning to understand how people with mental disorders eventually grow to hate their keepers, and that it would have been completely justified, under the circumstances, for Philip to believe I was an agent sent for no purpose other than to thwart and torment him. But whenever I asked Lucia about her two sons—aged nineteen and twenty-two—about whether either of them had mentioned anything about moving out of *her* basement so that she could keep her promise to take Philip for a while, she would cough and mutter about GMATs or LSATs, or GPAs not being high enough, or about the boys "keeping their expenses down to save up for a mortgage." And when I tried to fix a date for her to visit, she'd say, "Maybe Saturday. I'll check with Bruce and call you back." Then I'd remind her of how much she was owing on the amount required to keep Philip in food and clothes, how tired I was of looking after him, how, when Mother passed away, we'd agreed to share the burden instead of returning him to that home where Philip had tried to kill himself.

Sometimes I wouldn't have noticed that Philip was listening to our phone conversations, and I'd hang up to find he'd wriggled into the crevice between the refrigerator and the wall of its alcove, where I kept the broom and dustpan and garbage bags and extra dishrags, his face looking out at me as if I were responsible, as if it was my fatigue that kept Lucia from visiting him. And even though he hadn't said this (hadn't, in fact, said anything) I would have to agree, peering into the dark space from which he stared out, teeth bared, too deep for me to reach, his eyes piercing me to the bone. Speaking gently to him, I would promise to try harder next time, to sound less sombre, more inviting, though what Philip really wanted was not so much to hear our sister's voice, much less to enjoy her company, but to have me say something positive about him being there, in my kitchen, my basement, my life, something to the effect that our relationship wasn't—on *my part*—just so much responsibility. He wanted to hear that his friendship brought me, *at the very least*, the sad pleasure of sympathy. But it was exactly this that I could never bring myself to say, the two of us standing there, Philip backed as far as possible into his corner and me making up excuses about how I'd forgotten to tell Lucia about *Straight, No Chaser*, the Thelonious Monk documentary we'd watched, or the fascinating research Philip was doing at the library, or the many letters we'd worked on.

And this is how I gave in to his wish to send the letter to Monk's estate. I still remember the day we did it, Philip hopping around the kitchen in maniacal glee, then pausing by the rain-flecked window to hold his chin like some incurable nostalgic. I'd gotten us all suited up the previous Saturday, and together we'd gone to the library and copy centre, binding his "report" in Mylar and Cerlox and hunting down the correct mailing address. All there was left to do was slip the report and covering letter into an envelope, address it, lick the tab, and put it into a mailbox.

Naturally, it was the last of these that most worried me, since I did not want Philip's package to actually reach its destination. But there was no way Philip would buy my idea that he stay home rather than come to the post office in the rain and risk getting a cold, especially since Philip had a superhuman immune system, and could dance naked in a thunderstorm without getting so much as a sniffle, whereas I was always in bed with a chill, or walking around with my nose raw from tissue paper, or asking him, over and over, whether his prescription of antipsychotics didn't also confer resistance to viruses and bacteria. "You're the one who's always sick," Philip would say. "Maybe *you* should stay home." And, so, feckless as always, I had no choice but to let him accompany me, slipping an extra envelope into my pocket while he went to get his coat, then trying to hit upon all those subjects (well, hats) that would fully distract him, getting him more and more excited about how happy Monk's beneficiaries would be to finally have the pianist's madness explained, about all the ways they'd thank Philip for his research findings. By the time we got to the post office he was so hopped up I had no trouble drawing his attention to a poster and then quickly posting what I thought was the wrong envelope.

It was only when we got home that I realized that, in my own haste and excitement, I had sent off exactly what I didn't want sent.

You can imagine the anxiety that followed. The idea of Thelonious Monk's descendants and heirs bringing litigation against Philip and me, on top of the stress of having to go to work five days a week while leaving Philip at home with a caregiver, plus the general fatigue of not having anything to listen to, evenings, except his craziness, made me call Lucia again. "Oh, hello, Owen. It's great to hear your voice!" As usual, she was so pleased to hear from me it was as if we'd never spoken in our lives, though, as usual, her voice dropped from ecstasy to exhaustion when I told her we needed to meet.

"You did what?" she said, putting her coffee on a table in Mike's Diner. I repeated what I'd said and she leaned back and tilted her head at the ceiling. "Have you gone crazy, too?" she asked, after a minute, bringing her eyes back level. I told her how I had to hold my cup with both hands to keep the tremors from sloshing the coffee out; how I spent nights walking to the door that led to the basement and Philip and then walking away from it, circling through the upstairs rooms in the hopes that some friend had slipped in for a visit; how I'd taken to recording the pains in my body on a sheet of paper, noting that the headaches outnumbered their nearest competitor, aches in my lower back, by about twenty to one. When I finished, Lucia shook her head and recommended I see her "therapist."

"You have a therapist?" I asked. "What would you possibly need a therapist for?" I shouted, ducking my head when the other customers looked our way.

Lucia pretended to be affronted. "What do you mean?" she asked. "You know how hard it's been on me, knowing you and Philip are stuck in that house, and that I'm prevented, by circumstance, from doing anything to help you? It affects me, too," she whispered. "You have no idea how something like that gets to a person. Gnawing at her conscience."

And how could I reply to *that*? A hundred responses flashed through my mind, all of which would have made Lucia stop providing the little assistance she did provide: the occasional warm dinner delivered by one of her sons, the quarterly (it was supposed to be monthly) financial help, her willingness, as she said, to be always "just a phone call away" in case I needed someone to "dump on." In fact, even telling her that I understood, that I sympathized, didn't seem right, since agreeing so vehemently would have cast a bit too much light on her performance. So I just nodded and smiled and patted her hand.

"Here," she said, reaching into her purse and pulling out a card. "Why not give him a call? Say I recommended him. He's really helped me deal with the guilt. Most days I don't feel it at all." She patted her breastbone, roughly over the spot where the heart would normally be. "He's pretty radical in his approach. I mean really weird—in an *attitude* kind of way. But he's helped me accept the fact that there's only so much we can do in this world. He's really helped me be happy in *myself.*" I looked at the card again, wondering what dark magic my sister had met with. "He could do the same for you, Owen, if you really open your soul to him. Remember," she said, "it's about having faith—faith in *yourself.*" She stood and checked her watch. "I've really got to go," she said, "Alfred has hockey practice tonight, and Bruce can't drive him because the Rose Bowl is on TV." She looked at me, and I couldn't help but note the waiting in her eyes, as if she were readying to pounce if I said so much as one word about how Alfred was twenty-two and should be driving himself (if he hadn't crashed his own and then his parents' cars four and five months ago), and that, for God's sake, Bruce could miss fifteen minutes of football. But I smiled.

"Oh, before I forget," she said, reaching into her purse. "Here's the money you asked for. Sorry it's so late." And just then, as Lucia leaned over to snap her purse shut—perhaps as a result of the harsh overhead light—I saw, for a second, how terribly old she'd become, though I would not say this was something she wore on her skin, not the effect of the wrinkles around her eyes, the blemishes on her cheeks, the grey hairs poking out from under her mass of dyed hair. Rather, it was in the movement itself, the way she bent, making so little effort to peer into her purse that it was less an action than a lessening of resistance, as if there was a vast weight pressing on her from above, one that grew more apparent when she walked out of the café, the tendons of her neck straining to achieve the attitude she wanted to project.

I spent at least five weeks taking out the therapist's card and putting it away again; five weeks while my headache swelled to the point where its boundaries seemed to exceed the confines of my skull; five weeks while every nerve in my body prepared itself for the response to our letter, and the inevitable trauma it would cause Philip.

Finally, unable to take it, I dialed the number for Franklin B.M. Manchester, registered therapist, Ph.D. in psychiatry, etc. The secretary who picked up the phone had a slight lisp that sounded so much like my own I thought she was making fun of me, and it was some time before I could decide whether to respond to her questions or to point out that I had no interest in "humiliation therapy." By the time we got around to fixing the date of the appointment the only slot available was "three months from last Tuesday," so I agreed to go on standby, which meant working my way up the list and being willing to come in whenever time became available, or lose my place and have to start from the bottom again.

When I did eventually get in, Dr. Manchester was not at all what I expected: one of those tall, wiry intellectuals who have about them a manner of practised calm; who look as if they've spent years in front of a mirror, learning how to sit so that their bodies betray not one single mannerism. Neutral as ducks.

Instead, Dr. Manchester was more of a monkey. He was that animated, nearly jumping out of his seat when I came through the door, grabbing me by the hand and leading me to one of two barstools that sat in his office alongside a raised counter, while he went over to an espresso machine and made us some coffees. "Sugar?" he asked. "Cream?" And when I told him who my sister was he nodded and said, "Oh, God, I'm so glad to meet you. What a gem of a person she is!"

Despite this forcibly sunny disposition, I got to know as much about Dr. Manchester over the weeks of my treatment as he got to know about me. And I was always astonished to find him a little sadder each time we met, so that by the end of the period it felt, in meeting him, as though I'd run into someone on a park bench, one of those unfortunates who have lost so much they've abandoned all need for pretense, not caring whether you like them or not. Naturally, this wasn't an immediate observation, but one that developed over time, and maybe he simply realized, through careful questioning and observation, that this was the right tone to take with me, realized from that first introduction that too much exuberance was exactly what I *didn't* want. So maybe it was still an act after all, though the only thing I can say for sure is that his advice was, without a doubt, the worst I've ever received.

"Some days," he would say, "I have a hard time just getting out of bed in the morning." This was six weeks in, long after he'd memorized the fact that I took two sugars in my coffee, and milk if there was any, but never, under any circumstances, cream. I always had this odd sense when I walked into his office that he'd just stepped out of the demeanour I expected from psychiatrists (see above) and that his meeting with me was in fact his "break," a chance to let down his guard and just relax (which is why it was always such a shock to get the rather huge bill his secretary sent at the end of the week). Near the end of treatment it was *me* fixing the coffees, while he just sat there, doling out advice in a voice so melancholy his sentences were mere shadows of assertion.

"The trick, I keep telling myself," he would say, "is to think a lot less about what the exterior world is doing, and concentrate a lot more on the interior." He tapped his chest as though he were recalling a homeland from which he was forever barred. "Because it's inside where the drama lies," he snorted. "You know what the difference is between seeing the parade pass you by and seeing the parade coming at you?" I stopped in the middle of stirring three sugar cubes and two ounces of cream into his coffee, thought for a moment, muttered something about optimism and cynicism, realized they weren't really opposites, and was about to speak again when he interrupted. "The difference is in whether you've arrived on *their* time or *your* time. You know what the difference is between standing on a street looking up at the windows of an apartment where there's a party going on and actually being up there?" I muttered something about being outside, in the first case, and inside, in the second, and he rubbed his eyes with a thumb and forefinger and nodded solemnly, saying, "Exactly, exactly," then, "Do you see what I'm getting at?"

I brought him his coffee, which he thanked me for with a nod of the head, then settled on one of the barstools and began sipping. "I think so," I said. "Are you telling me your problem is that you are always putting yourself in the wrong place?"

"Exactly!" he responded. "You know, I've been looking for a way to phrase it for a long time. So succinct." He muttered this last comment almost below the level of a whisper, and whistled softly afterwards, then repeated it to himself with a tick-tocking of his head to either side. "If I'm feeling like shit," he continued, "if I approach everything like a chore, if I see only disaster around me, then that's what there's going to be. Get it? The inside becomes the outside which only amplifies the inside."

"You've got to change your attitude," I said, almost getting off the stool. "But I've been telling you that for weeks," I said. "Weeks!"

"I know. But you know how hard it is."

"I sure do," I grumbled, settling back down and sipping my coffee.

We sat there for a while longer in silence, Dr. Manchester hunkered on the couch so that his big knees were almost up at the level of his ears, and he finally sighed and rubbed his eyes with the palms of his hands. Finally, he looked up, bleary-eyed. "Geez, here I am, talking about myself when we should be talking about you. How's life?"

"It's actually getting better," I said. "I think coming here takes my mind off my problems, and I actually go back with a fresh perspective."

"Well," he said, softly. "I'm glad *one* of us is getting something out of this."

...

At first, the thought of a return letter from Monk's estate became something I decided to face up to with stoic reserve. Then, slowly, it became something I could think about from a cold, fatalistic remove. But I still couldn't quite get to the next stage, the one where I would become mad enough to just take Dr. Manchester's advice and switch over, change perspectives, join in.

Then, one day, I found myself sitting on the back porch with Philip while he went on and on about what the letter might say. Once again, his words were building to a crescendo beneath me, until I seemed to be rising with them, carried up as if strapped to a spinning rocket, with no idea what I'd find once I tore through the sky. But instead of reverting to my usual state—reeling from vertigo—I found myself speaking words of my own, and not like before, when I'd played along, humouring Philip, adding my ideas to his while actually using sarcasm and condescension to keep myself grounded. This time I actually joined him in earnest, at first as a kind of test, to see whether I could keep up to him, but then in all seriousness, greeting everything Philip said with equal abandon, including his screed on the many ways he'd console Monk's family when they realized their patriarch had not *gone*, but rather been *driven*, insane. The things he would say and do to make them feel better: like repeating how good Monk had looked in those hats even if they had made him crazy; or that maybe the madness was what let him compose such "finger-snappin'" music in the first place; or that maybe they wouldn't have had such a loving relationship if he hadn't depended on them so much to keep him straight; or that, at the very least, they must have had some "weird and whacky" conversations together, including some real "gut-busting" laughs at the things he got up to when he was at his "nuttiest." By the time Philip had hit his maximum speed, that breakneck rush where he could hardly keep up to the words necessary to convey his thoughts, instead of slowing him down I was right there, adding my own stream of words, hoping the two of us could attain a vocabulary that would exceed his frenzy, breach the stratosphere, let us both float, quietly, in the silence of space.

Philip looked at me in panic as the two of us went on, spewing words at a rate no untrained listener could have followed. We kept at it for one full hour, the many conversations with Dr. Manchester giving me the endurance to match Philip's monologue. And by the end of it the two of us were jumping around the porch, near-hysterical with the ideas bursting from us. Then, finally, just as I was on the point of swooning, I caught Philip as he collapsed into a sweaty mass. His mouth was frozen in a smile but he continued murmuring while I carried him from the porch to his bed. For the first time in as long as I could remember, he slept through the night.

Later, in the kitchen, drinking brandy to ease the dryness of my throat, the tightness at the hasp of my jaw, I reflected on the strange and improbable things Philip and I had come up with regarding Monk's hats. It was the richest conversation I'd had in years, and it occurred to me that all along it had been here, these fantastical things Philip routinely came up with, and which I'd exhausted myself trying to ignore. With only a slight shift in my disposition things that once irritated could now revive me, as if talking to Philip could resurrect parts of my mind long gone out of use—my imagination, to be exact.

I looked around the kitchen, then at the stairs down which I'd just carried my brother. I had always enjoyed descending to Philip's basement suite, though I had concealed this from myself by acting the part of the outraged landlord. Philip's rooms were never the same rooms twice. Never. They were a mess, a swirling chaos of overturned furniture, mismatched lampshades, magazines, books, and papers arranged in oddly symmetrical shapes that shifted by the day, piled and laid along the floor between rooms as though he were using them to build and rebuild that view of the horizon his underground rooms denied him.

And I went downstairs that night and lay down on the ground, as Philip did, and traced with my eyes the undulations of the line made by those books and magazines and toys and shoes and bits of careful garbage, wondering how it would read tomorrow. I looked around the place and saw how different it was from the way I arranged things upstairs, always with an eye to efficiency. Here, things came and went, shifted around, in through the window, out through the door, so that you not only didn't know where anything was but also didn't know what you owned in the first place. And I wondered if that arrangement suited Philip, because it seemed that each day for him was something of a mystery, demanding, because nothing could be found, that he make his plans on the spot, that he confront time in unforeseen ways. My days, on the other hand, were the same, the same, the same—planned and prepared for weeks and months and years in advance.

When I told Dr. Manchester about this epiphany, he only smirked and took out a handkerchief and wiped the corners of his eyes. "Well, that's it, then," he said. "Shit." I glanced up from my coffee. "I don't mean that in a bad way," he murmured, lightly wringing his hands. Then he looked at me directly. "You remember I told you when you came in here that I'm not one for 'interminable therapy.' I'm here to help people get to the point where they don't need me anymore." And I understood. "I'm going to miss you," he said.

But outside his office I didn't feel like I was going to miss him at all. And it was only some blocks later that it occurred to me, with a sudden and overwhelming disquiet, that it would sure be depressing to receive nothing from Monk's estate but a polite, indifferent reply, which, I now had to admit, was probably the best we could expect. Now, instead of being released from the paranoia that had haunted me since I'd slipped the wrong envelope into the mailbox I was overcome by an anxiety no less vicious. Now I was worried that we'd get *nothing*, that they'd dismiss Philip's letter as the ravings of a lunatic and throw it into the trash. And if getting back a negative response, or, worse, the threat of legal action, would devastate him, what would happen if there was no response at all? Whatever evidence the report was of Philip's obsession and craziness, it was also his attempt to communicate with the world, suggesting he was not yet fully lost, that he still believed there were points of view, forms of existence, even worlds, other than his own. Would receiving no answer seal him off once and for all, finally convince him there was nothing outside the confines of his skull?

I dithered with this for days, maintaining my new attitude toward Philip whenever he was around, pushing myself on, inventing elaborate fantasies, trying to match him delusion for delusion. But I couldn't help but see him slipping away, squatting down by the mail slot in the front door and flipping up the little lid to peer out, moving his head quickly to the side when the mailman slid through another load of bills and flyers. But instead of looking at the mail he would ignore it entirely, as if it was no longer the mail he was interested in but rather the world outside, which, for all its horrors—the people and cars and dogs and buildings—was becoming more and more preferable to the house he was trapped inside.

Whenever Philip heard my footsteps approach he'd turn and scoot downstairs into his basement suite, eyeing me suspiciously all the while, leading me to believe that he thought the response from Monk's estate had already arrived, and that somehow I'd gotten to it before he had, and hidden it away. I tried to counter this suspicion, as I then perceived it, by rhapsodizing about what the letter might contain, all the golden expectations it would fulfill, how Philip's name would find its way into biographies of Thelonious Monk, histories of jazz, scholarly essays. But the more I went on, the more bewildered and skittish Philip became.

I have to admit that playing insane wasn't as much of a chore as I thought it would be. There was a release in it. Sometimes I would find myself in bed at night, or on the bus to work, or in the supermarket, coming up with ideas that would delight him, some of them so imaginative they even delighted *me*. I felt as if I suddenly understood where Philip was, in a land of so many possibilities that the ground was constantly shifting under his feet; and while it wasn't a place I could get him out of, it was, I felt, a place where I could join him, providing company.

And this, I guess, is how I found my way into the second-hand hat store. I'm not sure whether it was something I had planned to do or whether I was just walking down the street one day, saw the sign, and decided to go in. I say "I'm not sure" because, in retrospect, the idea had been on my mind for some time—putting together a package that would do justice to Philip's expectations, that would give us a good excuse to celebrate—but I had not allowed myself to think of it as an option. Sure, I had play-acted and sympathized and even encouraged Philip's fantasies, but I had yet to do anything truly dishonest.

The proprietor nodded when I described the hat I was looking for, telling me it seemed to be "coming back into style," which didn't at all surprise me, having seen kids on the streets decked out in all things 1960s. He found one immediately, and threw in a box for free.

When I got home I found that Philip had, as usual, quickly run downstairs, as was obvious by the fact that the television was still on in the living room, there was a glass of half-drunk lemonade on the armchair, and the couch cushions were still warm. I put the box on the kitchen table and called to him, "Philip, come up! Mrs. Venderbeeck phoned today. She said a box had been delivered to her by accident."

Philip came up the stairs slowly, throwing his hand ahead of himself on the banister and pulling the rest of his body after it, moving so reluctantly he might have been *en route* to his own execution. When he reached the top step I pointed to the box on the table, but every time Philip tried to train his eyes on it they would veer away, as though my package scared him, or he wanted to resist it. When he managed to get them settled I noticed he was staring at the table leg underneath.

I turned quickly and went to the table, picking up the box and bringing it over, practically skipping in my excitement. "Look," I said. "It's what you've been waiting for." I pointed to the return address. "They've replied to your letter!"

Philip touched the box lightly with his finger, and drew his lower lip between his teeth. Then, with the tip of that finger, he pushed the box away, holding it at arm's length until I stepped back. "It must be some mistake," he said, though I got the sense that what he really wanted to say was, "You're lying."

I looked at the box. "What do you mean? It's what you've been waiting for!"

"I already got a letter from them," he said. At this, I snapped to attention, and for a moment considered denying it all, telling him the arrival of the box repudiated the letter, that Monk's beneficiaries had reconsidered whatever they'd written, that they wanted to take it all back. For a moment I thought of opening the box and pulling out the letter I'd forged, along with the grey fez from the second-hand hat store, even putting it on my head and running over to the piano to play "Epistrophy" as best I could, or do an impersonation of Thelonious Monk in one of his eccentric moods, where he'd do pirouettes, or walk in wide circles about the room, or mumble a few words nobody was supposed to know, a private language composed less of syllables than tones.

"I got the letter four weeks ago!" said Philip, emphasizing how late it was to be playing a trick on him, though there was something else in his voice, too, a keening note, as if it was taking all his resistance not to grab the box and give in to the temptation I was offering. "They thanked me for my interest in Monk," he said, pulling the letter from his pocket and unfolding it to read, " 'But due to the overwhelming amount of mail we receive regarding our sorely missed father and husband and friend we are not able to reply to every correspondent, though we want to assure you that this has nothing to do with the quality of your writing nor the nature of your concern.'"

Philip glanced over his shoulder, into the basement whose darkness was crowding him so badly he teetered on the threshold, and then looked back at me, his shoulders thrown against the blackness below, as if it was only being kept down there because he was blocking the stairs. "I didn't want to tell you," he said, looking sadly at the box in my hand. "You get so crazy when we talk about Monk. I didn't want you to be disappointed." He put his hands to either side of the door frame, and in that instant I knew that his standing there, his extended arms, were a protective gesture meant for me rather than himself. For Philip's desire to be down there, back in the basement, had nothing to do with returning to some magic kingdom (as I had imagined it to be), and everything to do with keeping that disorder from mounting the stairs, pushing its way to where I was, to where Philip had always needed me to be.

And it was then I realized that the letter from Monk's estate, the one held trembling in his hand, was, like the box held in my own, a hoax—one concocted by Philip to make me confront my own lie, and thus to end this business about Monk and his fez once and for all. He'd been carrying that letter for so long, crumpling it in his pocket, softening it, wearing it away, while he waited for the moment he knew was coming, when I would carry my performance too far and force him to step in, denying himself the illusion he so desperately craved so that he might prevent his madness from swallowing us both.

I let the box dangle from my hand, and nodded, acknowledging that all along I'd been defining what he was going through by what *I* was going through, by seeing him as my opposite: so that if I was the one looking out for him, and he was the one looked after, then what for me was responsibility was for him release. But it was not that at all—not release—that Philip was experiencing; rather, it was his own vanishing, as the disease ate away at what he was, putting something else, another person entirely, in his place. You see,

Dr. Manchester had been wrong: it wasn't a matter of perspective at all. On the contrary, there was no perspective.

"I'm sorry, Philip," I murmured.

He gave a half-smile then, and looked carefully at me, and at the box, and finally at the alcove beside the fridge. He seemed to catch himself in that moment, preventing himself from thinking or doing as he was prompted, because I could see the effort it cost him to shut the door to the basement behind himself, as if that instant of lucidity was all the agency he had.

His door has stayed closed ever since. And he no longer joins me for dinner, no longer wanders in hoping to hear me say something hopeful into the telephone, no longer crawls into the alcove between the wall and the fridge. I can hear him cooking sometimes, and I know he eats because I often wake up in the morning and find the fridge empty, the pots and pans of food I left on the stove scoured clean. The one time I dared open the basement door I found myself facing a wall of books and magazines that had been piled from the top step to the ceiling, preventing entry. Nor do I have any desire to go down there, having invaded Philip's space far too much already, preferring to wait upstairs while he goes through what I hope are the necessary preparations to restore our friendship, and which he's confided to Lucia, the few times she's visited, "are well underway"—whatever that means.

There are, as you may know, a number of great scenes in that documentary on Thelonious Monk, *Straight, No Chaser*, where you can witness the musician's eccentric behaviour. It always comes up in the context of questions regarding his music or his inspiration, some reporter or fan asking him about why he plays the piano the way he does, or the technique behind his compositions, or the relation of his music to, say, that of Dizzy Gillespie or Charlie Parker or Coleman Hawkins, and Monk will begin to spin and murmur and describe wide circles about the room, the smile on his face showing both amusement and pain. In the end, it's impossible to say exactly what he's thinking or feeling, or what, if anything, he might have to say—as if the only response adequate to questions about his music is to do something as incongruous as that music itself, as if it's very important that we—all of us—understand the vast difference between what we seek, and what we find.

The Man Who Came Out of
the Corner of My Eye

FOR WEEKS I'd been seeing him criss-cross the hallways of my home. At first, I thought maybe it was Lucinda, come to claim another stick of furniture (which would have been difficult, given that she'd already taken everything), but when I turned to look there was never anyone there. And yet the figure seemed so definite, so clear, from the shine of his shoes to the cut of his suit to the flapping tail of his overcoat.

My wife and I had had an argument. I was sitting in the breakfast nook the night we celebrated my fortieth birthday, toying with an antique metronome Lucinda had given me, when she stopped in the midst of clearing away the plates and champagne glasses to say, "You know, I find it a bit disturbing how you didn't want me to invite anyone to this."

I slowed the metronome as far as it would go, and set it aside, ticking softly. "I guess I'm not keeping in touch with much of anyone these days," I said, pretending to be thoughtful.

"That's what I'm talking about," she said. And by the sound of her voice I could tell she wasn't just speaking of the friendships—some dating as far back as childhood—that, in the last few years, I'd been slowly breaking off, but about the way I'd taken to living in my own home with my own wife, walking the halls with such careful steps, it was as though I was hoping to get by her unnoticed.

But because this was a subject I hoped to avoid, I instead told Lucinda I didn't like Katie McIntyre's second husband—the Baptist—who said that he, like Christ, never judged anyone, and instead just felt a deep and abiding pity for the Roman Catholics, homosexuals, and communists who didn't realize how hot it got in hell. I told her I couldn't stand the way Evelyn Moberley would call me when she'd decided to sober up again (for the twelfth time in the last fifteen years), apologize for being out of touch, and then promise to treat me better. And, finally, I told her that Joe Bolez, no matter how old a friend, should have known that telling me my compositions were "mediocre" was just plain offensive—even if, as he claimed, art demanded that he tell "the truth."

I added that I had realized something else about myself: I was the pathetic sort of person who didn't like being made fun of— even *gently*—but who took great delight in making fun of every-one else. Recently, I had come to recognize the hypocrisy of this position, and had decided to remedy it by avoiding the kind of intimacy that makes our friends so effective at annoying us, and us so effective at annoying them; and if the price I paid was no longer being intimate with anyone, then fine.

Lucinda waited patiently for my tirade to end, and then, her hands wrist-deep in soapsuds, responded, "Katie McIntyre only makes you speak to her husband when you call because she wants everyone to get along so that *Katie and you can get along.*" Lucinda was looking down into the suds, and when she wiped her forehead left a trail of bubbles there. But she was too preoccupied to notice, as if she had something else on her mind than what she was presently speaking about. "As for Evelyn Moberly," Lucinda con-tinued, "she's an addict. Not right in the head. And I think it's dis-graceful of you to abandon her to this sickness. And I don't care how often she needs you to prop up her illusions, or forgive her for being out of touch, or pretend you 'understand' when she decides to stop using antidepressants, because they're drugs too. She's sup-posed to be your *friend*, for God's sake!"

She stopped what she was doing at the sink and reached for one of the dishtowels to wipe her hands, her eyes snagging on the remains of my birthday cake as though she was shocked to find it there. "As for Joe Bolez," she whispered, saving her voice for some-thing else, "he's a composer, and I guess that makes him as weird as you. Maybe Joe is a bit blunt sometimes, but he's also given you a lot of support over the years. Or have you already forgotten the referrals and introductions that helped you get some of your stuff put on? Maybe you're just bitter because he always teases you at the wrong time, and because he's so merciless about it. Or maybe you're just mad at him because you never have any good comebacks."

"But never mind all that," Lucinda said, her voice rising almost to a shout. "If we were perfect we wouldn't need other people. What I want to know is this: if you're planning on ditching all your old friends, then what about me?" Here, there was a terrible pause (which I blame on my rather sluggish emotional reflexes) before I said, "You'll always be my friend."

And she replied, "The fact that you have to lie to me proves we are anything but."

I came to miss Lucinda not because she'd been my friend, but because she'd been such a great acquaintance. Marriage and friendship, to my mind, don't go together very well. But marriage and acquaintanceship? Let me explain the difference: friendship is transparent, an intimacy so intense that the two friends seem to coexist, as if their selves have overlapping boundaries. Acquaintanceship, conversely, is founded on distances. It is ruled by politeness, by the respectful awareness that the other person is not an open door, that their agenda is not known to you; and this, as far as I am concerned, is marriage more or less: the co-habitation of two *individual* agendas.

I'm not talking about big secrets—affairs, murders, former marriages kept under wraps—though these certainly can be part of it. What I'm talking about are the microscopic evasions: about how much of your day at the office was actually spent working (versus the amount spent having coffee or afternoon beers); about how much dope you're smoking ("just an occasional toke, dear," versus several joints per week); about what your train of thought really is ("no, dear, I never look at other women," versus the lurid fantasies continually playing on the screen of your mind). Marriage is the accumulation of lies so inconsequential unto themselves—these things you hide from your wife to avoid friction—that only together can they possibly be dignified as falsehoods. But they do amount to a separate existence. And since the best marriage is one where you can live more or less as you prefer while still appearing to participate in harmonious compromise, the happiest couples are almost always acquaintances masquerading as friends.

Lucinda wanted us to be real friends; I haven't seen her in over two years.

When she left—as I said—she took everything, without so much as a word of protest from me. Afterwards, I dragged in one of the old lawn chairs, mended it with twine, and set it next to the book-shelf and the small, portable stereo I'd bought after she took the European unit that had made recordings of my music sound better than they really were. She also left me the piano, since I needed a means of livelihood in order to be able to make the alimony payments. Very soon, I would sell the house; but for now I was just basking in the emptiness, having realized that what I liked most about a home—*any home*—was walking in and imagining how it *could be* outfitted. It was this imagining that I liked; once the place actually *was* outfitted, I was invariably bored. So I spent a lot of time, in those two years, sitting around and exercising my imagination. I wrote a suite of songs called "Empty Chamber Music"; it received moderate reviews.

This emptiness, however, didn't only extend to my home. I seemed to be divesting myself of everything, not only friends and furniture, but also entertainment, conversation, even food. It was hard at first, giving up the gourmet meals Lucinda had prepared, downgrading to canned soup, sandwiches, green salads, or going down even farther, from three meals a day to two, cutting out snacks, but the truth was I simply had no desire to eat, and the feeling of emptiness, the lightness in my stomach, made me feel oddly powerful, as if I were floating free, no longer tied down, able to give up anything at a moment's notice. Yet, it also made me tired and lightheaded, as though something were missing, a crucial blood flow.

During the weekends—when I wasn't at a recital or at my studio or at a practice—I would walk out into my backyard, into the scintillating motes of light, into a garden gone wild with flowers whose seeds had drifted in from the neighbourhood, and just sit there, enjoying the quiet. And it was here that I had contact with the only two people to keep me company, outside of work, during those first years on my own. One of these was Fred Macklesmith, my neighbour of ten years, whose hand would occasionally dart above the fence and flutter there, waving at me. And I would think, eureka!—the perfect friendship: a hand waving for a few seconds over the top of a very high fence *and not expecting me to wave back*. The other person, whose name I don't know, and who only visited me once, was a local man I'd seen before: middle-aged but boyish, probably autistic, or born with significant parts of his brain missing. He used to speed-walk up and down the street, his hands raised to his ears to block out the laughter and jeers of the local kids—some as old as sixteen—who harassed him whenever he came through the neighbourhood—copying his awkward movements, trying to trip him up, calling him names. One day I simply opened up my gate to give him an escape, and he came into my garden, wandering through the tall grass and looking at the flowers, picking up fallen apples, as if he'd never seen a plant or fruit. I remember because it was the time of moths: that yearly infestation, near the end of summer, when the backyard, and everything in it—from the grass to the trees to the lawn chairs—is coated in tiny white insects, their wings folded up, all of them awaiting some directive to arrive from east or west, instructions on where to fly next. He spent a lot of time running his hands lightly over the tips of their wings, setting off flurries of moths that would resettle just a few feet over. That afternoon, in his presence, I felt as if I were witness to a sanctity that made for better company than any I'd experienced—even that of Fred Macklesmith.

But after two years with Fred and the singular encounter with this nameless man, I began seeing things, or, rather, I began seeing *a thing*. I don't remember exactly when it started, but I know that eventually, some time in autumn, it became routine for me to be doing something—slicing bread, say—and to suddenly see a figure in an overcoat calmly strolling down the hallway. But when I turned to look, there was never anyone there.

After a while I began to see him not only in my house, but in other places as well. I'd see him sitting on swings in the park as I walked to my studio. I'd see him in the passenger seat of the car rented by the local symphony so that I could get to and from rehearsals more quickly. I'd see him leaning on the bar at O'Toole's when I went down there for my weekly night of whisky obliteration.

I hate to admit it, but I grew used to this hallucination, thinking it was probably how my conscience appeased itself over the way I'd ditched my wife and friends. And I was prepared to let my conscience take care of itself. I had better things to do with my time.

But after a while I grew frightened, since—let's face it—it wasn't normal to be seeing people only at oblique angles; and this fear, as it always does, turned to fascination, especially once I noticed that this figure seemed to be beckoning toward me, trying to say something, though he'd always be cut off in mid-sentence, disappearing the second I turned to take in what he was saying.

What happened was this: I trained myself not to look at him directly. It's a very difficult thing to do, actually, to pay attention to something that's in the corner of your eye, out of your focus.

The first time I was really successful at doing this was in the spa of the Delta Hotel, which I went to every Sunday afternoon after a hard half-day of musical notation. He was sitting on a bench against the wall behind the Jacuzzi, and I trained my eyes very deliberately on the foam and bubbles around my chest and let him inhabit the corner of my left eye. After a while, he smiled at me, then reached into the pocket of his overcoat, pulled out a handkerchief and mopped his forehead, which had grown sweaty in the heavy steam coming off the bubbling water. "Bit hot in here, no?" he said.

"Depends on where you're sitting," I replied, concealing my astonishment under a forced, casual tone.

"I'll meet you outside when you're done," he said, and rose up and walked away. Naturally, when I turned to look for him he'd disappeared.

By the time I got out he was waiting for me in the lobby, sitting on one of the complimentary chesterfields and sipping an espresso. I sat on the easy chair positioned at ninety degrees to the chesterfield.

"How are you, Jeff?" he said.

"Never mind that," I replied. "Who the hell are you?"

"I have a job proposition for you."

"I already have a job."

"Not like this one."

"Well, that's obvious," I trembled.

"I think it would be a good idea if you took a break from music for a while. You're not really getting anywhere with it anyhow."

"Thanks," I said, rising. "Thanks a bunch."

"How do you expect to grow as an artist," he replied, "if you run from the truth?"

He sounded like Lucinda, who had always assumed I thought I really *was* talented, that the world was unfair not to give me the recognition I deserved. But by thirty-seven I'd already experienced enough years of rejection—starting with having to perform a *second* audition before making the high school band, and progressing through two decades of lost competitions, bad or mediocre reviews, rejected grant applications, and the stinging words of Bolez—to know that I was going to be a composer even if there wasn't a grain of evidence to support my decision. It was my right to hope, goddamn it, even if 90 percent of the world thought I was a hack.

And who was Bolez not to support me in this? Who was his loyalty bound to, some abstract notion of aesthetic value or his friend? After all, great art would still be produced—the Beethovens of the world would still exist—whether or not he humoured me and said my stuff was great as well. Why not let time be the one to sort good from bad? I'd be dead by then, and it wouldn't matter a bit whether every single note I'd written had been flushed down the toilet.

Me, I'd always told Bolez his stuff was good even when it was shit, told Katie and Evelyn they were leading meaningful lives even when they were not. This was why my friends loved me—why they'd sounded hurt and disappointed and surprised when they'd called to ask why I'd been out of touch. I'd always supported their illusions, and just couldn't understand why they'd so poorly supported mine. Lucinda was right, Bolez had helped me in the way of introductions and favours; now, if he'd just refrained from teasing me about how "banal" my stuff was we'd have gotten along just fine.

I was about to launch into this rant—surprised by how much I wanted to say all this miserable shit, as if it had been waiting to burst out since I'd cut everyone from my life—except that I realized it was my wife and friends who should have heard it, not this weirdo in an overcoat. So, instead, I said "Goodbye" and walked out of the hotel.

Later that night, I was trying to figure out whether I was hungry when he walked in, looked around, and leaned against the nearest wall.

"You should get some more chairs," he said.

"What for?" I asked.

"What about guests?"

"There's only me." I took a gulp of air against the rumbling in my stomach, and decided it was enough.

"So here's the deal," he said. "I've become involved in a little business enterprise, and I think you're just the man."

"What the fuck are you talking about?" I asked.

"I've decided to start up a new business: breaking up friendships. And I think there's a lot you could teach me. I mean," he said, "the way you did that thing with Katie McIntyre was just amazing." He whistled and shook his head in pure admiration. He was, of course, referring to my usual modus operandi, which I call the "gradual withdrawal method." This involves a slow slackening of the ties of friendship, the sort of thing where you always let the answering machine get the phone, then don't return the message for three or four days, then a week, then ten days, and before long a whole month—citing some vague "business" that kept you from responding; with letters or email I would let an even longer initial period go by, say six weeks, then eight, then twelve, and so on, and my responses would grow colder and colder, more stiff and formal, filled with astonishingly boring anecdotes about the weather; the state of my shoes; a minutely detailed account of how inflation has outstripped, cent for cent, the federal pension plan; and so on. Nonetheless, it still took me three years to get rid of Katie this way.

Such is the strength of friendship.

"You're a pro," he said, shaking his head. "A total pro. The two of us could make buckets of money." And here he outlined his plan, beginning with the sort of clients who came to him: people all haggard and twitchy, obviously beset by unwanted company, and looking for some way out of the friendship short of violence. "You've been out of practice lately, but I don't think it would take you long to regain your winning form," he said. "I mean look at your record. For years you treated your best friends like shit. *Years.* They liked you so much they were willing to put up with being snubbed over and over and over again! You've got something special, son. People are attracted to you. They form attachments."

He continued: "You know what I think it is? I think it's because you're weak. Because you never stand up for yourself. Never come back and actually confront them on how they've hurt you. It's easier to just stop seeing them. And that makes you perfect."

I couldn't help but nod here. He was right: I was a weak person, unable to withstand honesty, and unable to force a confrontation. I'd tried to change this, to fight back, but Bolez—being, as Lucinda said, quicker and sharper—always got the better of me. Alternatively, I'd tried to just follow my natural tendency to give without receiving, to support them without being supported in turn, but it was too hard. There was still the nagging voice of pride telling me I was being taken advantage of. I was, as he said, perfect.

His plan was to bring me in on the ground floor, as a full partner. He would meet the clients, figure out their needs, and then he'd come to me. My job was to go over to the client's place, meet the friend they wanted to get rid of, work hard at winning his or her affections, and then, once the unwanted friend was fully hooked, once they'd stopped being friends with the client in order to be friends with me, I would turn on them quite suddenly, becoming cold and distant, and ultimately cutting them free as only I knew how. For this, we could charge upwards of fifty dollars an hour, plus GST and PST, and could probably write off most of our expenses as tax-deductible overhead. It was, the man who'd come out of the corner of my eye said, "a win-win proposition."

I took another gulp of air. "Let me ask you a question," I said; and when he nodded, I continued, "Are you on drugs?"

"I was, but I found Jesus."

"Okay. Get the hell out of here." But as I turned to stare at him, forcing him to disappear under the directness of my gaze, I caught a last glimmer in his eye, a cold and ruthless attachment, so intense that it made me feel as if he'd crawled right into my body and taken up residence. It was such a creepy feeling I never wanted to look at him again.

Which meant, of course, that before I knew it he was back.

As early as the next morning he was there, sitting on the edge of my bathtub as I brushed my teeth and stared out the window, his legs, encased in a sharply pressed pair of pin-striped trousers, dangling over the rim. "You know what I've decided? I've decided that if I'm going to go off drugs, then I'm going to go off *all* drugs. The doctor's prescribed me these antidepressants. He says they stop the obsessive-compulsive cycle that brings me back to narcotics. But, I mean, what's the difference? Coke. Antidepressants. They're both chemicals in my brain. They're both drugs. If I'm going to go clean, then I should go totally clean, don't you think?"

"There's a difference between narcotics and medication," I said. "Maybe it would be good for you to try a different drug for a while, you know?"

"I don't see the difference," he said. "It's all chemicals."

"Well, maybe you shouldn't make generalizations. Every drug is different."

He stopped swinging his legs and sat up straight on the edge of the bathtub. "Jeff, I know I've failed you."

"No you haven't." I stopped brushing my teeth. What was he talking about?

"No, I've failed you. So here's what I propose. I'm going to stay sober for one whole year as a way of proving my friendship to you. Until such time as I've proven to you that I am clean we will have no contact. . . ."

That was it. Something came over me then, and instead of going for my usual diplomacy, I snapped, "Hey, don't draw me into this twisted thing."

"But . . ."

"I am not part of your addiction. You understand? I will not be your substitute fixation."

"You don't understand."

"Oh, I understand."

"You're no friend of mine, Jeff."

"No?"

"No, you're not. You're not worth being sober for."

When I got downstairs to the kitchen I found him standing there with a spatula in his hand and a fresh carnation in his lapel. Breakfast was on the table, already prepared. He wished me bon appétit, and then asked whether I'd given any more thought to his proposition. I told him no, not really, but my voice was less assured than it had been the day before, and reluctantly I took a bite, but only one, out of the best scrambled eggs I've had since Lucinda left.

I saw him the rest of that day. He was up in the west balconies at the recital hall, dangling his feet over the edge of the railing and riffling through his wallet. He was in the restaurant, sitting with an older woman who had had a very bad facelift, both of them sending the waiter back to the kitchen time and again with their meals, and finally turning to me (they'd chosen a table right beside the one my agent and I were seated at), saying "I can't believe you eat in this place." I tried to ignore him. "He eats in this place because you like to eat in this place," he said to my agent, Ed Morton, who, at first, seemed not to be aware of him. But when he started saying things to him like, "Don't you find Jeff just a little too accommodating? He'd shine your car for you if you got him just one night at the Met," Ed found it impossible not to pay attention. I didn't get it. Wasn't this guy just a figment of my conscience? Ghosts are only supposed to be seen by the people they're haunting, aren't they? Or can ghosts just do whatever they want, appearing whenever and to whomever they please?

When he saw that the salt shaker I was using was empty, he got up and walked over, handing me the one from his table. I had just been buying for time, appearing to do something with my food in order to avoid eating it, but this new salt shaker solved both problems, because when I tried to use it I found that the top had been unscrewed and a heaping of salt poured out over my food. "These composers," the man who'd come out of the corner of my eye laughed, standing by our table, "all idiot savants. Wouldn't recognize an old trick if you played it on them a hundred times." My agent—being the greasy type who represented second-stringers such as myself—wasn't used to being flattered by being invited to join in the humiliation of someone else (usually, he was the one being humiliated), and so was soon laughing, and inviting the man who'd come out of the corner of my eye, and his aged lady friend, to join our table, both of them nudging me with their elbows every time a joke was made at my expense, expecting me to be a good guy and laugh along. This went on for forty minutes before I finally turned and stared at the man who'd come out of the corner of my eye; and, again, in that second before he disappeared, as I looked at him, I felt that horrible sensation of being violated.

When I got home the laundry had been done, the stove cleaned. And as I went to sleep I could feel someone running his fingers through my hair and singing a lullaby. I yelled and howled that he stop, but the singing went on until I was finally, between shouts, worn down into a fitful sleep.

By the next morning, he was back, but alone this time. He was holding up a newspaper, reading aloud from the first section: "'Cassandra Davis and Marlene Holden are willing to take the fight over adoptions for gay couples right to the Supreme Court.' Oh God," he said, "could you imagine growing up with those two for a mother and a father, or rather a mother and a mother, or, *rather*, a *father* and a *father*," he snickered at his own joke, and then shook his head sadly. "You know, sometimes the Holy Spirit is a long time in descending upon these sinners. But God must have his reasons for keeping them in the dark. God always has his reasons." He shook the paper, folded it up, and moved behind me as I sat staring at the blueberry pancakes he'd prepared; and he began massaging my shoulders. "You know that anything is possible for the Holy Spirit. It says so in the Bible."

You're completely demented, I thought.

Then he went on about how the Bible was the word of God. I pointed out to him that if this was the case then God must suffer from a bad stutter, since there were as many Bibles as there are Christian sects.

"Well, *I* read a version that was prepared by a group of Christian scholars from various denominations in Lyons, France, in 1969." He stopped massaging me, reached into the satchel, pulling out a version of the *Good News Bible*, and began reading from the introduction. "They left out a few books included in other versions because they were redundant."

"Oh yeah," I said, snickering. "So what used to be the word of God is now redundant. Last year's writing by the Holy Spirit is this year's redundancy. This year the Old Testament books, maybe next year one of the Gospels. Don't the Gospels just repeat each other? Is the word of God that unstable?"

"I got you a present," he said, changing the subject.

"Please," I begged. "No presents." It was bad enough that he was making me breakfast—not that I would eat it.

"Do you need a ride to work? It's on my way."

"No!"

"We could be a great team."

"Go away!"

"Oh, as long as I make food and give you a massage and sing you to sleep?"

"I don't care about those things."

"Yes you do. You just don't know how to take the bad with the good."

"I don't want any of it."

"Just being honest," he shrugged. "Why can't you love me?"

Infuriated, I gazed directly at him, and this time he seemed to slip entirely out of my field of vision, scuttle off to the side, and pass up my cheek to the corner of my left eye, where I could feel his little hands taking hold, as if he were crawling inside. The only way to stop the feeling was to turn my head in his direction, at which point he would reappear off to the side, and the feeling would stop for a minute or two, and then begin again.

"Excuse me, sir?" It was the investment counsellor. I shifted my head again and looked at her. Then, after a minute, I shifted my gaze away, looking somewhere else. The man who came out of the corner of my eye kept reappearing and I was trying to make him vanish. "Excuse me, sir? Sir, are you all right?" Yes, yes, I nodded my head, and then looked behind me. "You have to sign, sir." Every time I looked down at the mortgage papers, it took me forever to read past the rows of figures and fine print, the debit and asset columns, the various brackets and categories pertaining to the condition of my house and payments to date, and then he would be there, at the edges of my vision, asking questions: "Hard day at work?" "What did you spend all your money on?" "Don't you think you're smoking too much dope?" "See the tits on that teller?"

When I flashed in his direction he'd be gone, and then I'd have to grip the pen and go back to the form until, finally, unable to even sign my own name without his interference, I turned from the counsellor and rushed out of the bank, with her yelling at me from behind and waving the paper in the air.

It was hard to run while looking all around to make sure he kept vanishing, keeping my gaze fixed on no point and every point in particular, wishing I had the eyes of a fly, that I could see in every direction at once, that there were no edges to my vision. And, finally, after I had been running for some time—and after I'd tripped and fallen, and been helped up by strangers whose hands I shook off—I passed a horse and carriage, one of those tourist attractions that take you around the historic downtown. I stopped and looked at the horse, standing there, the bluebottles buzzing around it unnoticed, its blinkers set sharply against its cheeks, its quiet expression suggesting it was blissfully lost in the solitude of tunnel vision. Inspired, I put my hands to either side of my eyes, reproducing the effect of those blinders; and with that the man who'd come out of the corner of my eye finally disappeared.

I was three blocks from home, walking this way, when the kids saw me—the kids who'd chased that autistic man into my garden—and nudging one another began to follow, whispering at first, then pointing, then opening their mouths to yell insults and to laugh. After that I felt a rock hit my back, someone stepping on my heels, then my hands. And all I could think of was how badly I wished I were in my home, far away from them, and from everybody else.

Last Notes

ON A COLD MONDAY in the winter of 1995 a nurse unwound the bandages from around Felix Frankenbauer's head, and the composer walked unassisted for the first time since the accident, staggering to a piano to find he could no longer write musical notation. Recalling the scene, I see Frankenbauer pause above the blank sheet music, pen in hand, utterly bewildered, as if what the nurse had pulled from his head was not a bandage but rather a spool of memory tape, wrenching it out, fist over fist, exasperated at its length, ripping, balling, and dropping it into a dirty bucket. In truth, however, this image is the effect of hindsight, my mind doubling back on itself, for what I really saw was Frankenbauer pause above the paper, and I thought nothing of it. And for the next six months he fooled us—pretending to write music while actually filling page after page with nonsensical scribble—though he must have known we'd find out eventually.

But even if this had been the loss it first appeared to be, Frankenbauer would have had nothing to complain about. For the better part of thirty years he'd been a leading composer, internationally recognized, his many recordings stocked in the sections reserved for classical music. There were symposiums devoted to him; prestigious labels bidding for his performances; crowds at the door—young and old, fund raiser, fan, student, peer—whom I had to turn away in my capacity as "second assistant to Felix Frankenbauer." I would tell them, yes, it was reasonable to want "just two or three minutes" with Frankenbauer, but could they imagine if he agreed to every such request? He'd have no time for music. And I was made crazy by the way they clearly understood this argument, but refused to accept it, demanding "just a second" of the composer's time, as if, in the end, they couldn't have cared less about new music issuing from Frankenbauer; as if the music he had already created was only there to establish him as an authority so they could get his endorsement for their projects. Inevitably, it would reach the point where I would have to tell them he *was* and *always would be* unavailable, threatening the truly persistent with the police.

Yes, Frankenbauer had reached the pinnacle, and so I believed he had less reason to complain than other men who, late in life, might have lost significant portions of memory after being struck on the head, repeatedly, by the roofs of their cars as they flipped end over end down an embankment.

It was like watching a man who wants desperately to live being driven to suicide. He never said anything, never complained, nor did he take it out on his staff, either through verbal abuse or mass layoffs. Instead, he spent a lot of time at the piano, trying to satisfy the conflicting demands of a world that recognized his genius, and a genius besieged by that recognition. I watched him lose months of his life striving for a solitude he hated; and, watching this struggle, I grew angry at a world that, having heard of Frankenbauer's accident, and suspecting his imminent death, grew more insistent than ever.

In the end, it broke him. If only they could have been happy with the few hours he set aside each day for appointments. But the instant he opened a slot on his schedule the door would be flooded by people who'd heard he was seeing visitors. By then, Frankenbauer was too sick to manage that kind of crowd, though he saw them anyhow, driven to it by the suggestions Tomlinson planted in his head (part of Tomlinson's efforts, I am sure, to sabotage the old man's career). All of this meant that Frankenbauer had to stay up into the night, needlessly weakening himself, in order to satisfy his urge to create, playing into the morning while all the staff also stayed awake, ears pressed to the walls, listening to a music so unlike anything he'd done we came to believe the accident had jarred something loose in him—a late flowering of genius that put all his previous masterpieces to shame.

I had never heard anything like it. The notes veered off in every direction, as though repelled by one another, as though the last thing they wanted was to unite in harmony; and yet there was music there: an odd, dying call, as if persecution (if such a thing is possible) had its own scales and chords, its own whimper before the process ran its course. Shortly after the bandages came off, Frankenbauer would play for hours, his hands moving in fits against the keys, the look on his face suggesting he was as surprised as we were by the curt rhythms, the jarring notes—the sound of a talent trying to erase its signature. Within days, however, his face settled into a relaxed, content expression, and he no longer held his hands as though they'd been taken from someone else and sewn onto the ends of his arms; so that for a short time before the headaches started—before his decline and death—he played music, perhaps for the first time since he'd sat in front of a piano, as if it was exactly what he intended.

He was also making marks on paper by then, though had we seen the pages we would have all rushed for tape recorders. What Frankenbauer played was different every day; our mistake was in thinking it a single piece being worked to perfection. And, so, I suppose there's some truth to the accusations made by Horace Grober, writing in *Contemporary Classical Magazine*, that we—by which he means the staff present for Frankenbauer's final compositions—are in some way culpable for the loss of the music. But while Grober is correct in seeking to blame *somebody*, he is wrong to indict anyone other than myself.

...

I wonder how Henry George Tomlinson feels these days, the music legally in his possession, scrawled across a thousand pages in a code so arcane Grober wastes whole columns lamenting the failure of musicologists at decrypting it. And Grober's not the only critic who feels as if he's stranded on a desert island with nothing but crates of gold to eat; more than a few of them think nostalgically of the days they might have put Frankenbauer in a headlock and squeezed the information out.

The truth is, I never paid much attention to Tomlinson. Not at the start. By the time of the accident a staff of at least five was needed to manage the house and business—from cooking and cleaning (and later nursing), to royalty payments, corporate bookings, interviews and articles, and organizational commitments. The staff consisted mainly of music students and minor composers, since Frankenbauer could never turn away anyone in need of a temporary home and quick cash.

Some thrived under this system: exchanging their labour in return for instruction (which the old man was too generous in providing), cupping their hands around the sparks thrown off by his blaze of genius. These usually stuck around a few years and then left to start their own careers.

Others hated the old man. Having taken too long to realize their lack of talent, they were unable to imagine a life other than serving Frankenbauer, who then became the source of their considerable despair. (This was, of course, completely false, since any of them, at any time, could have embarked on new careers; and while I saw much during my time with Frankenbauer, the only thing worse than these artists who, in losing hope, had not lost their passion, was the artist who, having reached the pinnacle of expression, realized there was no one out there truly listening.)

Funnily enough, I wouldn't put Tomlinson or me in either category. In my case, I had stood a little too close to Frankenbauer's genius, and while all that light had exposed my deficiencies I had decided, rather than growing embittered, to attach myself to his glory, helping out where I could, and maybe, in the process, earning myself a well-deserved footnote in the biographies (which was far better than most people ever got).

Tomlinson, by contrast, had served Frankenbauer longer than anyone, but despite having his musical ineptitude continually demonstrated had somehow not lost faith in himself as a genius, filling up score after score with his horrific mediocrity long after most people would have just gone over to hating Frankenbauer full-time.

You should have seen the condescension with which he greeted Frankenbauer in the hallways, the perfectly paternal smile he'd flash the old man upon hearing his latest composition, the way he spoke of Frankenbauer when he wasn't present, telling reporters or scholars or house guests that, "Indeed, Felix does produce some very *pretty* music." You should have seen the care he took with the old man, as though he were made of eggshell, but careful to stay just this side of exasperating, so that Frankenbauer would never have the opportunity to turn to him and shout, "I'm not that fragile, you idiot!" (Not that Frankenbauer would have ever reproached anyone.)

As for his own compositions, Tomlinson never mentioned them. And this, finally, is why I think he's crazy: even the most confident of failed artists, no matter how pious in regard to fame, needs some affirmation of his or her work. But with Tomlinson you got nothing. *Nothing.* And the only clues to his continued output as a composer were the scheduled performances at venues so tiny they went unlisted in the schedule at the back of the local arts bulletin, and (as I would witness the night I finally opened his door) the stacks of scores cluttering his room, running around the walls right up to the ceiling. The man who continues to create art in the absence of any audience—or even the opportunity to *speak about it*—is the sort of individual portrayed by models in catalogues for psychiatric equipment.

...

The image I have—of Tomlinson getting up from his desk one day, wandering to the workshop for a pair of wire cutters, and then crawling under Frankenbauer's Saab to sever the brake lines—is, of course, the work of theory. Nobody witnessed the accident, though the car was found by Tomlinson, who that afternoon, for some reason, had decided to go for a "brisk jog," happening to run right along the only ridge for miles around, a narrow road that he alone knew Frankenbauer would be driving on that day. He called the ambulance. He helped haul the composer's battered body from the wreck. He rode all the way in to the hospital and stayed there two solid days, being removed only on the advice of doctors, who worried he might be suffering from dehydration. And you should have seen Tomlinson at the first anniversary of Frankenbauer's funeral, as he walked solemnly, utterly full of himself, up to the podium to perform his horrendous "Dedications to Felix Frankenbauer": tall and thin, his eyes closed, chin tilted up, jaw knotted, and his right hand set, as it had been ever since the accident, as though it should have been holding a pair of wire cutters.

But I'm getting ahead of myself.

When Frankenbauer came back from the hospital he was disoriented, confused, having lost control over several portions of his brain. His care was primarily taken over by Tomlinson, who seemed more attentive to the composer than ever (Frankenbauer had no wife, his sexual inclinations running the other way).

Almost immediately things started happening. I don't know how Tomlinson did it, but he managed to convince the old man he'd been a bastard prior to the accident, so that Frankenbauer would come down into the kitchen, see me, and say the most ludicrous things:

"Erno, I think it is time that you contacted the women whose children I have, for all these years, been refusing to recognize as my own."

"Erno, I think we should discontinue our policy of turning away from the door the illegitimate children I have fathered."

"Erno, it is time, don't you think, that I finally revealed to my adoring critics the name of the composer whose work I've been plagiarizing all these years?"

"Erno, I do not think I have been nearly proactive enough in making contributions of my money and, more important, time to all the arts boards, charities, and organizations."

"Erno, I would like to apologize to you, to all the staff, for the years you've had to endure my bitchiness; for the shoes shined and re-shined; for the shirts ironed and re-ironed; for the scores copied and re-copied—in short, for my perfectionism."

And I always replied in the same way: "Mr. Frankenbauer, sir, I'm sorry, but I haven't the faintest idea of what you're talking about. You've always been the greatest of employers to work for."

He would look at me as if someone were being tortured in front of him, and he'd shake his head and pat me on the shoulder, turning around so that I too had to turn away, or else witness the soft spots in the back of his skull where the crumpled roof had punched holes in his cranium.

From then on, Frankenbauer became a magnet for every kind of parasite: women—whom I'm sure he'd never met—claiming support for non-existent children; people who bore no resemblance to him claiming that he, their father, had abandoned them at birth; musicians not worth a cent arriving to point out the various passages he'd stolen from their work; an endless stream of administrators demanding his name on various petitions, his presence at various functions; the rest of the staff claiming all kinds of exemptions for stress leave, demanding bonuses, telling the worst sorts of sob stories in order to squeeze from him a few more dollars per hour. Frankenbauer grovelled in front of them as if he really did need to make amends; as if he should have cared one second for the self-respect of people who not only didn't deserve any, but who also would have contributed far more to civilization, justifying their births even a bit, by piling their dead bodies around his home as a barricade against others just like them.

Even then I knew how this sounds, how it reads on the printed page, how it seems the work of an "unreliable narrator" whose blind worship of Frankenbauer makes him miss that the composer really *was* a monster; that Frankenbauer and Tomlinson actually *were* lovers; that it was Tomlinson who wrote the compositions Frankenbauer then "tweaked" to world fame; that this story is about art—*Tomlinson's art*—as the purest of expressions: done neither for fame nor money nor societal betterment, but out of a selfless love.

But while I appreciate the conclusion reached by this twist on Frankenbauer's story, it was Anton Fischer (good old Horace Grober's foil), not me, who invented it, a critic who, writing in *Avant Garde* at the height of the controversy following Frankenbauer's death, suggested that Tomlinson was the only person who deserved to inherit the Frankenbauer estate, since he had been the real genius behind the old man's compositions in the first place, as proven by recent performances of work "held, for the first time, under his own name." Fischer argued that what Tomlinson and Frankenbauer had gone through, as lovers, was so claustrophobic, so oppressive, that no one had the right to even think of calling Tomlinson into question. For as long as the controversy lasted, Fischer held that Tomlinson had, in an ultimate proof of love, totally sacrificed himself to Frankenbauer's fame, and, as a result, had created a music "so imbued with the beauty of that sacrifice" that the notes "could barely contain it."

To this day there are a number of people so convinced by Fischer's argument that they want every recording by Frankenbauer recalled, and the whole catalogue reissued with the name Henry George Tomlinson at the top.

Except I was there that night, standing beside the piano, and I know.

Frankenbauer motioned to me from his bed. I put down the tray containing the tea and the six different painkillers for the head-aches resulting from the accident. I came over to where he rested on the pillow, his strands of grey hair spread against the sheets like tributaries on a map.

"Help Frankenbauer up," he whispered.

I did as asked, and then we stood there, beside the bed, his head hanging loose on his neck, my feet shifting, uncertain of where to go. He wanted so much to move in a particular direction, but it had taken everything just to ask for help; and, with the choice left up to me, I had no better guess than to guide him to the piano, which was exactly what he wanted.

"Lift his hands onto the keys," he said, his voice so hard and yet so quiet that it reminded me of a shard of glass worn smooth. Then, once I had done this, he said, "Open the folder. Papers. Pen." I opened the folio resting on top of the piano and took out a few sheets of unlined paper covered, to my surprise, with a disorgan-ized pattern of squares and triangles and snaky lines, and, as well, I took out a pen, placing these to the side where Frankenbauer might reach them. Then I lifted out the sheet music underneath and put it on the stand, noticing immediately that the handwriting on it was not his.

Flexing his wrists, he began. It was the first time since the acci-dent that I'd been able to watch him play, and I was surprised at how he moved his fingers along the keyboard, at how he doodled geometric shapes here and there on the paper, placing them in what seemed to me an arbitrary fashion, as if he had enough strength to lift the pen but not enough to determine where it

Last Notes   169

would fall. His head hung so low it seemed the tendons were no longer servicing his neck. And again I had the sensation that these were not his hands at the keys, their manic vitality so at odds with the limp arms to which they were attached. "Don't want to play his music anymore," whispered Frankenbauer, hammering the ivories. "Don't want them to think they're *his* notes." But I didn't understand what he meant, since the music he was playing was not the one on the score in front of him—the one written in Tomlinson's crabbed handwriting—and which Frankenbauer never so much as glanced at.

And it was then, in that room, listening to a music whose beauty seemed a side effect of its slow decay into noise, that I first thought I'd figured out what Frankenbauer was doing, though I continued to just stand there, listening until the exhausted composer slumped down on the stool, and then, raising his head, spoke into the polished black wood: "There must be some way to undo what he's done." I wanted to grab his head, to draw him away from the keys, because his gaze seemed less to rest on the piano than to want to hammer its way into it, to punch the sort of holes the car roof had punched in him. Slowly, I came around and lifted him, light as bone, back into bed.

He made no motion of resistance, and within seconds seemed to have fallen asleep, but when I moved to go he groaned, turning to look up at me. "Please?" he whispered, and as I bent to him he put his arms around my neck. "Frankenbauer's all alone," he whispered, holding on to me with a grip that was, I guessed, his last refutation of weakness and defeat, of a darkness he knew I could not see, and I had to kneel on the bed or completely lose my balance and fall against him. Frankenbauer continued to pull at my neck, and I continued to struggle, not so much to get away, but to find a position that would make him content, struggling with him as though I were a wave, a water in which it was possible for him to float only by lying very still. And then I was whispering, his twiggy legs and ribs lying flat against the side of my body, his head rising and falling upon my chest. Before his eyes finally closed he murmured something like "Thank you, thank you; you will get paid; Frankenbauer thanks you; your money's coming." It was a goodbye or a promise, though less addressed to me than a distant angel, a quiet remark at the end of some other episode.

"You're welcome, Mr. Frankenbauer," I said, lying there in the dark, reaching up to touch his head.

I was there the better part of an hour, moving his body off mine inch by inch, an agony of contortions where I sometimes had to hold myself in one position for minutes, every muscle tense, even holding my breath to keep him from waking up. But he never did, giving me the chance, once I'd gotten out from under him, to take that score, as well as the sheets he'd written on, off to the photocopier in the nearby office, and then put everything back into place.

In my room I spent ten minutes rapidly paging through Tomlinson's score, confirming that Frankenbauer was neither playing it backwards, nor taking it apart, but rather *resisting* what it was attempting (Tomlinson's derivative effort to sound like Frankenbauer), and, somehow, in the process—despite his brain injury and half-paralyzed body—creating art. Next, I picked up the pieces of paper on which Frankenbauer had made his own notations, wondering whether the old man knew that his attempt at resistance was itself a composition of total originality, and therefore noted it down the only way he could. I thought, mistakenly, that it must have been the source of considerable despair for him in those days, realizing in some part of his mind that he was creating the greatest piano pieces of his career, pieces that no one would ever be able to play.

I spent the next several days downstairs in my room with these photocopies. (I'd returned to his study and rifled through the piano stool, the filing cabinet, his night stand and desk, duplicating everything I came across.) But while I thought I had managed to cross-reference Tomlinson's score with the coded one Frankenbauer had written that night in his room, I would not be sure until I'd applied my system to another set of the two composers' pieces. But I found only examples of Frankenbauer's compositions in the old man's study, nothing more of Tomlinson's, which meant I would have to steal them directly from his room.

It was my first and only time inside. As I've said, Tomlinson was quiet, leading a life of extreme privacy, and so I was not prepared for the extent of his compulsion, for the piles and piles and piles of compositions rising from the floor to ceiling, solid as pillars, some of them set so narrowly apart that only a man as thin as Tomlinson could have squeezed between them; for the carefully arranged record collection (oddly lacking even a single recording by Frankenbauer); for the blotting pad on the desk by his portable keyboard, so smeared with India ink it was like tar, retaining my fingerprints as they grazed its surface.

I was so amazed by the room, and by the thrill of cracking Frankenbauer's code, that I began searching through Tomlinson's manuscripts without even making sure I'd shut the door behind me.

But when Tomlinson walked in I was disappointed at how predictable it was, how I should have known he'd catch me. What was surprising, however, was that Tomlinson didn't yell, or throw me out, or even run out and make a report to security. He stared at me for several minutes, frozen in the act of hanging up his coat, and then walked over to the desk and slumped in his chair.

"There's no point," he said, making every effort at pity. "Even if you were to pass off one of mine as your own you wouldn't find a place or orchestra that would agree to perform it. My work," he gestured around the room, "*is too far ahead of its time.*"

"But I'm—I'm not . . ."

He made a motion as if brushing a few strands of hair out of his eyes, making the gesture over and over again, as would a person who's just walked through a cobweb. "You're not the first staff member I've caught doing this," he sniffed. "There's a desperation to this place," he whispered. "Except the old man, of course, who seems to be doing just fine with his delusions of grandeur." Tomlinson paused, and then said, "Well, he did before the accident. Have you heard what he's playing these days?" He shook his head. "He's gone from mediocre to worse. And I'm incapable of helping him."

"'Helping him?'" I glanced quickly at the scores I was holding in my hands, and while I again recognized Tomlinson's handwriting on them, they seemed entirely different, musically speaking, from the one I had found in Frankenbauer's room. While that piece had been bad—a shameless rip-off of the old man's style—these were worse for *not* being rip-offs. And then what Tomlinson was doing became suddenly clear to me.

But he told me anyway: "Yes, I sit him down every day, and I show him the kind of work he used to compose. His style, you know. It's ludicrously easy to reproduce. I put it down note for note, hoping he'll follow along, learn how to write music again. Poor old fool," Tomlinson shook his head, "he looks at the scores I've written out, and then launches into another rendition of that chop suey. It's all he can play now." He twiddled his thumbs. "Perhaps, in a sense, it's a just reward for having lived the kind of life he's lived. Hurting all those people."

I calmed myself by carefully squaring up the papers in my hand, returning them to the pile from which I'd taken them. I could only imagine what saintly endurance, what absolute patience, Frankenbauer drew upon during those endless hours with Tomlinson— even while dying, while time was running out, while there was still so much to do—sitting there day after day, and suffering the "instruction" of that lunatic. But before the thought could grow physically painful I blotted it out by asking a quick question: "Tomlinson, could I see these exercises you've made up for him?"

"Why?" he asked, sitting up, eyes narrowed.

"Well," I said, "I saw one on his piano the other day, and I was really impressed. You've taken Frankenbauer's style to whole new heights."

He stared at me a second, and then laughed. "Well, you've just confirmed to me what I've always suspected."

"What's that?"

"You're as bad as the rest. You couldn't tell a piece of music from a rock 'n' roll song." He tossed a folder of papers across.

Two days later Frankenbauer was dead of a massive brain hemorrhage. By then, of course, I hardly noticed, having become obsessed with my failure to verify Frankenbauer's code against Tomlinson's parodies. They just didn't match up; though that didn't stop me from trying to wring the answer from them.

As reporters stormed the door, and policemen and doctors marched up and down the hall; as the remaining staff tuned in to radio stations interrupting scheduled programming to play Frankenbauer's music; as television cameras showed up outside the front doors and the notables cried and told and retold anecdotes to the reporters; as all this happened I fled into the riddle, sitting at the piano and poring over Frankenbauer's scores, hitting keys at random to try and unlock that irreplaceable sound. In the meantime, while I was plinking in the key of G, the place was emptying itself out, many of the assistants and servants not willing to wait on instructions, packing up their things, accepting jobs elsewhere. And by the time the lawyers brought us together for the parcelling of the estate, there were only two of us left, myself and Bernard Coates, both so shocked and saddened by the composer's death that we'd gone on with the work—filing, answering the phone, dusting, collecting royalty money (much increased due to commemorations of his death), responding to lawsuits—as if they were rituals against grief.

I had never before seen the lawyer who was present that day, but he obviously knew what he was doing: racing through the formalities, recalling how he'd managed to shoo away most of the "false claimants" to Frankenbauer's legacy (those "mothers" and "sons" and composers he'd supported in those last, feeble-minded months) before putting on the videotape.

It showed Frankenbauer sitting up in bed, Tomlinson holding pillows to either side of his head. For a while the composer said nothing, staring fixedly into the camera as if he were the one doing the filming; then, finally, flicking his eyes in Tomlinson's direction, he said quietly, "Frankenbauer leaves everything . . ." Here his voice either dropped out of range of the microphone, or his mouth moved in absence of sound (though I could swear, by the movement of his lips, that he was saying "Frankenbauer leaves everything to Frankenbauer"). Then, the sound level rising, the composer concluded, "He leaves everything to him." And here he and Tomlinson exchanged glances, staring at one another as if they not only couldn't understand what had been said, but as if they had no idea what they were doing in the presence of one another. And then Frankenbauer looked back at the camera and said, with emphasis, "*He leaves everything to him! Him!*"

I could only reflect sadly on these two mental defectives dispersing an inheritance worth hundreds of thousands of dollars.

"It is clear," said the lawyer, turning off the video, "that Henry George Tomlinson is the sole beneficiary of Felix Frankenbauer's estate."

Coates and I looked at each other, but Tomlinson seemed even more alarmed by the news than we were. Even in his state of shock he managed to mutter something about "refusing" it, about not wanting to "live off the proceeds of mediocrity," about how it was his role "to starve, as all true artists must starve" (it obviously hadn't occurred to him that for the last twenty years he'd been doing just fine off Frankenbauer's earnings). The lawyer, however, was certain, and said we had a given period in which to contact our own legal counsel, should we wish to contest the evidence of the videotape.

After that meeting—as I was standing in the hall watching Tomlinson argue with the attorney—Bernard Coates came up and led me down the hall. "Well, what do you think of that?" he asked. I looked at him, baffled, doing something with my hands. "It was me who took that videotape, you know, on Mr. Frankenbauer's request."

"Not Tomlinson's?"

Coates went on, ignoring me, "There was no talking him out of it!" Coates seemed very bothered, and he kept pulling at his own shirt cuffs. "But that shyster's got it all wrong, I tell you! Mr. Frankenbauer wasn't right in the head!"

"Come on, Coates," I replied without much conviction, "he was weakened, and he couldn't read music, but it only got bad at the end."

Coates ranted on: "That shyster. He doesn't know what we know, you as well as me: after the accident Mr. Frankenbauer only ever referred to himself as if he weren't in the room. You remember. I think when he said he was leaving everything to 'him' he didn't mean Tomlinson; he meant his own self!"

"Are you kidding, Coates? How's a man to collect his own inheritance after he's died. . . ." I stopped in mid-reply, staring at Coates. He was right. After the accident Frankenbauer had always referred to himself in the third person. And it was at that moment that it became clear, and I turned away from Coates as he shouted after me, running down the hall to my room, where, in a single motion, I swept all of Tomlinson's parodies off the piano and grabbed Frankenbauer's cryptic sheets, hurrying over to my shelf to pull out the composer's "Piano Works: The Collected Scores." And there, with hands trembling so badly I could barely turn the pages, realized that the "he" Frankenbauer had referred to that night at the piano, the "he" whose music he was resisting, was not Tomlinson but himself. He had not, as I thought, been looking *into* the piano but *at* it, at his own reflection on the polished surface. That night, it was his own music he had been attempting to unlearn.

It took four weeks—during which I stayed locked in my room, only going out early in the morning, exiting my private entrance to grab a bite at an all-night diner four or five blocks off—before the rectangles and ellipses of Frankenbauer's code resolved themselves into readable notes. It was another week before my delight at being able to play the pieces gave way to remembrances of Bernard Coates, Tomlinson, and Frankenbauer's inheritance.

But by then it was over. Not that I could have done anything. The legal machinery, once set in motion, was too relentless. I exited my room to find the mansion completely deserted, all the staff and movable furniture gone, with only old Bernard Coates left to superintend the place prior to its sale. My presence must have gone unnoticed in the rush, the notes coming from my piano unheard amidst the reading of pink slips (mine was in the increasing heap of mail I'd been ignoring), the scrape of furniture, boxes, and feet.

Coates was the first person I met upon coming out of my room. He was so hurt by my absence he barely wanted to speak, though he finally did reveal that the majority of the estate had gone to Tomlinson, with a small portion left to the Frankenbauer Foundation, a trust fund intimated at in an earlier will, which Frankenbauer wanted set up to nurture young composers. Coates was certain this had been what Frankenbauer alluded to in the videotape. "Mr. Frankenbauer, he loved his music," said Coates. "I'm sure that's where he wanted his monies to go."

But I wasn't so sure. And when I looked around the place, wandering into the empty rooms, staring out of Frankenbauer's vacant study at the large "for sale" sign on the front lawn, I wondered how I could have become so lost—to both myself and the world at large—as to be oblivious to the place being emptied. But I had only to go back to my suite and my piano and Frankenbauer's pieces to understand how easily it had happened. The pieces were designed for such a loss: the self vanishing into the music, the logic of the score overpowering and erasing the intelligence of the musician. And while I have tasted such liberty before, performing the music of Bach and Chopin and others, there was to those performances the question of how I, the performer, chose to play, not to mention the style already embedded in the pieces, whereas Frankenbauer's late music seemed to negate the signature of the person playing it, and, especially, that of the composer himself.

As for Tomlinson, I saw him one last time. For a while, after Frankenbauer's death, his name was everywhere, speaking about Frankenbauer on the television or radio, with that condescension I am now sure was honestly felt, and which in no way interfered with or contradicted his affection for the old man, with the love he had put so visibly on display during his hospital vigil. And while there was no more talk of "living off the proceeds of mediocrity" (the lawyers had obviously sat Tomlinson down and pointed out the benefits—*for all concerned*—of him being in charge of the estate), there was even more about his own greatness.

For the short time that controversy raged around Frankenbauer's genius—by which I mean the squabbles initiated by Grober and Fischer and their respective allies—Tomlinson was much in demand, though he refused to corroborate either side, until both grew exasperated with how he always turned their questions toward his own compositions, and decided to argue it out without him. Eventually this died down too, as Fischer couldn't prove a thing without a witness, and Grober, in order to cement his argument, would have needed at least one recording, one performance, or one deciphered score of Frankenbauer's final piano works to prove that the composer's genius was so without precedent it obliterated any charge of plagiarism.

But I was not willing to provide. This is a great loss, I know, but in the end my loyalties to Frankenbauer outweigh any I might have to the public (whom, after all, I blame for his death). You see, to have played his late pieces then—to settle a personal grudge against Tomlinson and the critics—would have been to exploit Frankenbauer as badly as they had. Nor was I willing to see these pieces recorded or, worse, published, to provide royalties to an estate almost entirely in the hands of Tomlinson. For while I knew that Frankenbauer would have been happy to have his music bring rapture or relief to another, he would not have wanted it played under any circumstance where people might have heard his name in it. After all, they had been written not to increase his fame, but to ring through the mansion during those last, terrible months, distracting all of us from his slow death by enacting that death in the most consoling of music.

It was art as he had come to understand it: created not to exalt the artist, but to provide for another.

It wasn't until the anniversary of Frankenbauer's death that I came to this realization. Lost as I had been in deciphering the music, I missed the first, official funeral, at which considerable crowds were in attendance. But within a year Grober and Fischer had abandoned their argument, having so damaged Frankenbauer's credibility that the composer's stock sank below notice. (I am confident it will eventually return.) The world of contemporary classical music is fickle. In fact, the five or six people who showed up that rainy day in October were not there for Frankenbauer at all. Rather, they were there to see Tomlinson perform his "Dedications," impressed as they (and the critics) were by a man who, having finally gotten his hands on a little money, managed to arrange large-scale performances of his compositions, inviting just the right people, and creating such spectacles, that most of the world was now convinced there was something to him after all.

I was standing beside Tomlinson as the priest spoke, the two of us folding our hands, bowing our heads, and waiting. And then, when the words had ended, when we'd placed our flowers on the memorial headstone, when the attention of the guests brave enough to face the rain turned toward the piano in the nearby gazebo, Tomlinson turned to me and said, "Maybe there's something you'd like to play?"

I looked at him. He glowered back, so that I understood this was neither a dare nor a risk on his part—that he was so firmly convinced of his genius that nothing I played could in any way threaten him. And for a second I considered it: going up, stretching my fingers and wrists, and letting all the world know how great Frankenbauer had truly been. His reputation restored. Thanks to me.

And in a gesture that was at once an affirmation of Frankenbauer's artistic beliefs, and their eclipse, I turned back to Tomlinson, saying, "No, no. Go ahead. He would have wanted you to play."

Acknowledgments

Bill New looked over early drafts of several of these stories. My gratitude to him for this, and for much else.

Mária Lelkes went through my Hungarian spelling. Thanks are hers; any remaining mistakes are mine.

"Tales of Hungarian Resistance" appeared in *Northwest Review*; "The Inert Landscapes of György Ferenc" in *The Colorado Review*; and "Into the Ring" in *The McNeese Review*. The editors of journals such as these are the people who keep writers alive. Eternal thanks.

Simultaneously blunt and subtle, Phyllis Bruce is the best editor I've ever worked with. In every way, she made this a better book.

Special thanks to David Bergen. This wouldn't have happened without him.

Last, and most important, for Marcy and Benjamin, where home is.